i-genius A twist in the tale

i-genius A twist in the tale

50 BEST STORIES FROM I-GENIUS YOUNG AUTHORS HUNT

illustrated by

Archana Sreenivasan and **Priya Kuriyan**

Published in Red Turtle by
Rupa Publications India Pvt. Ltd 2013
7/16, Ansari Road, Daryaganj
New Delhi 110002

Sales centres:
Allahabad Bengaluru Chennai
Hyderabad Jaipur Kathmandu
Kolkata Mumbai

ISBN: 978-81-291-2933-8

First impression 2013

10 9 8 7 6 5 4 3 2 1

Contents

foreword

The book that you are holding in your hand is more than just a compilation of fifty interesting stories. This book is a celebration of young writing talent from across the country. It's a platform for children to demonstrate their writing prowess. While countless books are published in our country every year, one such as this is rare. I feel privileged to have been a part of this wondrous journey that Max Life Insurance embarked on with Ruskin Bond, Chetan Bhagat and Rupa Publications to identify promising young writers.

Max Life Insurance has a vision to provide financial security to its customers. Through our products and programmes like i-genius scholarships and i-genius Young Authors Hunt, we aspire to build a better future for this great nation.

If recognized at the right time and encouraged, talent of any kind can take children places. Every parent knows that children are storytellers at heart. Max Life Insurance i-genius Young Authors Hunt is a salute to these master storytellers. We believe this recognition of expression will motivate not just those children whose stories find a place in this book but many more who will enjoy these stories and feel inspired to write.

We are overwhelmed by the remarkable display of potential reflected in the thousands of stories that reached us. Some were emotional, a few autobiographical, lot of them were set in fantasy lands. I am sure you will appreciate the challenge the jury had to face to shortlist the final stories that you find here.

A book such as this is limited by its size. We could celebrate just fifty stories here. But I believe that each child who participated is a winner and my congratulations to every one of the 55,000 children who registered in the Max Life Insurance i-genius Young Authors Hunt 2013.

We have enjoyed reading these stories and hope you do as well. Happy reading!

Rajesh Sud
CEO & Managing Director
Max Life Insurance Co. Ltd.

a note

from ruskin bond

India is a land of festivals, and during the last two or three years we have added one more festival to our calendar of delights—the Literary Festival.

It all began in Jaipur, the pink city, and it has since spread to almost every town and city in a land hungering for intellectual nourishment: Mumbai, Kolkata, Chennai, Bangalore, Pune, Bhubaneswar, Goa, Agra, Allahabad, Travancore, Shimla, Kasauli, Mussoorie, the list is endless... And now even schools and other institutions are conducting their own festivals, even if literature takes a back seat to the general festivity.

All this activity has come about because in recent years, a number of young Indian authors have been making it big on the national and international scene. And in this era of television and Internet, successful writers soon became celebrities.

That means writing has, at last, became fashionable.

Is that why so many of you, boys and girls, have been ready and eager to take part in the Max Life i-genius Young Authors Hunt?

It has been anything but a hunt. Over 5,000 entries poured in, mostly online, and if anyone was hunted it was the judges, editors and jury members who had to read and assess all these submissions. Young authors were on the hunt, and they left us in no doubt that they are going to be the celebrated authors of tomorrow.

Fame is the spur.

Or so it is said.

Certainly when I was a boy with literary ambitions, I did dream of being a famous writer one day. No literary festivals in those far-off days. No book fairs or book launches over cocktails. My literary icons were Dickens, Barrie, Somerset Maugham, Conrad, Chekhov, Conan Doyle and P.G. Wodehouse. But they were 'invisible' authors. Their works may have been household names, but you never saw them in person, and their photographs seldom appeared in the press. No TV then, no Internet. A successful playwright like Barrie might take a bow at the end of the opening night of *Peter Pan*, and that was it. He would then return to his eyrie to write another play or novel. And the same with Maugham, who hated making public appearances.

When I was a young man of just nineteen in London, I was invited to give a talk on BBC radio on what it was like to grow up in India before and after Indian independence. While I was waiting to take my turn in the sound-proof studio, a tall, good-looking man in his forties came into the waiting room and sat down beside me. We exchanged pleasantries, mostly about the English weather and the coming Coronation (nothing very intellectual, I'm afraid) and then he got up and left. My producer came in just then and said, 'I see you've just met Graham Greene. He was here for a book programme.'

So the stranger had been Graham Greene, then probably at the height of his fame as a novelist. He had recently written the script for the film *The Third Man*, which was having a successful run in the West End. I'd read several of his books—and I hadn't recognized him! Had I known who he was, I would probably have been tongue-tied. But we had met on equal terms and had chatted about mundane things, like two normal people waiting for a bus.

How wonderful to be anonymous! Had he been the star in the film, he would have been recognized immediately. But one of the charms of being an author was that you could be 'invisible'—just another wayfarer roaming the streets in search of a story.

In search of a story...

For that, in a way, is what writing is all about. Looking for a story—and telling it.

The word 'authorship' usually implies writing a novel or a book of some sort. Those who write for films are script writers; those who write for newspapers are reporters. And so on.

When I was starting out as a writer, an author was someone who'd had a book published. Until that happened, you were just a writer. I remember when my first novel was finally accepted (after submitting three rewrites), my editor and publisher, Diana Athill, took me out to dinner and said, 'Well, Ruskin, you are finally an author!'

Sixty years ago, the standard advance for a novel was ₹50. This doesn't seem much today, but it was enough to get me back to India. I was going to take a chance and try to make a living from my pen, and that too in the country of my birth.

In London, I had made friends with a Vietnamese girl who was studying at the university. She was a lovely girl, gentle and very sweet. For fun, she used to tell my fortune with tea leaves. When you finish drinking your tea, you let the tea leaves settle at the bottom of the cup, and the pattern they form gives you an indication of what to expect in the future. I enjoyed these sessions because it meant sharing innumerable cups of tea with her, with whom I fell in love. But when I asked her to marry me, she said it was not in the tea leaves.

Well, chance gives and takes away and gives again. If I had married her, I might have ended up in Vietnam in the middle of a civil war, and India was calling.

It was March, 1955, and I was twenty-one years old. I had left India to seek my fortune in the west; and now I was returning home to find, if not fortune, at least fulfillment of a sort.

Although I had been earning a living for over three years, in many ways I was still a boy, with a boy's thoughts and dreams—dreams of romance and high adventure and good companionship. And I was still a lonely boy, alone on that big ship, sailing into an uncertain future. Thanks to all the great books I had read, I could write fluently and in a style of my own. But would writing sustain me?

I was carrying two books with me—Thoreau's *Walden* and Richard Jefferies's *The Story of My Heart*—both reflecting my growing interest in the world of nature, the natural world. At night, I would sit on the deck, under the stars, while the ship ploughed on through the Red Sea, bringing me home to India. And as I sat there, pondering on my future, a line from Thoreau kept running through my head: 'Lonely! Why should I feel lonely? Is not our planet in the Milky Way?' and I knew that as long as I responded and respected the natural world, I would never feel lonely upon this planet, and I would never be short of words to describe it.

a note

from chetan bhagat

When I was approached by Max Life Insurance to judge a contest for students, I was wary. After all, I didn't want to add to the stress of our already overworked students, making them work more and judging them for it. Any judging process involves not just selecting a few winners, but also rejecting a lot of enthusiastic participants.

However, the organizers assured me the contest was different. For one, it was a writing contest. Participants had to send in a piece of writing—a story or a non-fiction piece. We wouldn't be testing them on their course materials, checking their report cards or making them go through stressful interviews. They could submit an entry from home to begin with.

As a writer myself, I enjoy the process of writing. Hence, I felt this contest was giving children a chance to do something enjoyable, and create something from their imagination. The academic curriculum in our schools often has little scope for that.

The second exciting thing about this contest was the reward itself. Most contests give material prizes, or even cash rewards. While there is nothing wrong in that, but this contest offered something unique—the chance to be published. The winners were to be featured in a book published by a leading publisher, Rupa Publications. I remember from my early days of writing how much it meant to be published the first time.

The joy one feels the first time one sees one's name in a book is indescribable. To be able to be a part of a contest that would provide this felt wonderful.

So, here we are. This book has stories that managed to win the jury's approval. Hopefully, they will be enjoyable for you to read, too. Please note that we had thousands of participants, of which less than three per cent made it to the final cut. Of course, this also means many other good stories were left out. Hopefully, the participants who didn't make it will not see it as a reflection on their own writing, but a situation of too much choice. Also, we hope more than anything else that they enjoyed taking part in the unique contest.

We have also left some of the stories somewhat raw, and not over-polished them in the editing process, so they retain some of the charm and innocence that comes only from young writers. You may find that stories could be improved as well. However, do note the spirit of these participants and their considerable achievement at a young age.

I love stories, and I am glad many others do too. I am also delighted you picked this book up and you are giving these young students of writing a chance.

a note

from red turtle

What a wonderful ride the Max Life i-genius Young Authors Hunt has been! From more than 5,000 entries to the final fifty, we have read, evaluated, categorized these stories and essays, over and over again. The editorial team at Red Turtle went from being amazed at the sheer power of imagination to being thoroughly entertained by each and every piece that was submitted in the course of this competition. As people who work with words, we read hundreds of stories and novels and essays professionally, but the joy that came from reading these entries was a different experience altogether.

So what were we looking for during the judging process? We had a firm conviction that each writer is unique with his or her own way of expressing their innermost thoughts. We therefore looked for those pieces that had a completely new and different style or story to tell. The ability to stand out from the crowd with your words and imagination was a big plus. The second big tick from us came for those who had a sense of story—the ones who could build a piece in the space of 1,000 words and keep us hooked to know what happens next. And finally, the kind of language used. Yes, language can be polished and worked on, but that little spark in many stories where a turn of phrase added incredible beauty, or a piece of dialogue that brought alive the characters was what we looked out for—and found in ample measure in many pieces.

The final fifty stories that appear in this book cover an

entire gamut of styles and ideas. Some are imaginative, others are full of action and adventure, and yet others are thoughtful pieces on family, friends or the environment. Reading these stories had us believe that the future of our society rests in the hands of bright, imaginative, conscientious, thoughtful children. From concerns about the environment and the aged, to showing one's love for grandparents and parents, to out and out imaginary worlds, these writers are engaged with the world around them in many ways. It was our endeavour to find the most promising voices from among so many and put them together in this book. The stories appear in this book in random order and are not a reflection of any ranking. Also, as editors, we have retained the original voices as well as the writers' styles so that the innocence and freshness of the plot lines and descriptions are not lost.

To each writer whose story appears here, congratulations, you are well on your way to being an author. For all those who wrote and whose stories do not appear here, congratulations, because you have entered the world of imagination and books and writing, which we think is a pretty good place to be in!

Year 1 of the Max Life i-genius Young Authors Hunt was fun and intensive. We look forward to more stories and more madness in Year 2. A programme as large and complicated as this needs many people to work behind the scenes for it to be a success. We'd like to acknowledge Pooja Sodhi of Max Life Insurance here for her cheerful support of the Red Turtle team at all times; Dibakar Ghosh of Rupa Publications, who held the process together from our end; Maithili Doshi Aphale, Raj John, Sohini Pal, Anita Yadav, Rebecca Sarah John and Tanya Sharma from Red Turtle's design and editorial team, who gave this book its finer touches.

We hope our readers will appreciate and enjoy these stories—for who knows, we may meet some of these writers again in the pages of their own books sometime in the future.

Sudeshna Shome Ghosh
Executive Editor, Red Turtle

mr donut's dream world

Riddhi Singh, Age: 14, Jhansi

I heard something—a shrill, loud, annoying sound—awfully close to my ears. Maybe it was coming from my bedside table. Yes, definitely from my bedside table. The slow processing of my lazy brain told me that my alarm was belting out its monotonous ring. I sat up straight and grabbed the clock. It had been ringing for fifteen minutes! I got out of my bed and ran to the bathroom. I was not a morning person and to get ready for school in the morning I kept a margin of just twenty-five minutes. Today I was going to be late. For the third time in a row.

I dashed down the stairs as fast as my legs could carry me. My mother was eyeing me the whole way. Before she could say anything, I snatched my lunch from the table. Unfortunately, she grabbed my hand.

'I don't have time for this, Mom.' I struggled against her strength.

'You should realize what a pain you are becoming. Today's the third time. We'll be embarrassed by your principal again,' she said with her eyes narrowed.

I finally broke free and said angrily as I ran for the door, 'Then kick me out of the house.' Only silence followed. I knew my words must have hurt her, like they always did. But my mom was the kind who didn't keep grudges. She moved on pretty fast. That was the only thing I liked about her. Had it been been any other parent, I would've surely been grounded for a whole year.

I pushed her out of my mind and prepared myself for my teacher's wrath. But when I opened the main door I saw something similar to what Alice must have seen when she peeked inside the rabbit hole in *Alice In Wonderland*. But this was not a hole. It was a long, dark tunnel. I looked at it in confusion and then turned around. Behind me, the living room and my mom had disappeared. It was pitch black. With no other way out, I stepped into the dark tunnel.

The tunnel was endless. I had no idea how long I had been walking when I saw a tiny point of light at the end. I increased my pace and ran towards the light. By the time I reached the source, I was short of breath. All I saw around me were trees. Not green trees but trees in as many colours as you could think of.

'Is anybody here?' I shouted and immediately I sensed motion. The next thing I knew, there were rabbits all around me. There were so many of them it was creepy. I started backing away.

'No. Don't move.' That was enough to make me stop dead in my tracks. A rabbit on my left had spoken and soon every rabbit started shouting, 'Don't move! Don't move.' They were freaking me out so much that I don't think I could have moved even if I wanted to.

Finally, they all stopped shouting and stared at me.

'She's the first human he has ever dreamt of,' someone in the crowd muttered.

'Where am I?' I asked awkwardly.

'You are in Mr Donut's dream world,' the rabbit on my left said.

'What?'

'This is Mr Donut's dream world. Everything he dreams of comes here,' one of them said.

'That doesn't make sense.'

'It never will,' the rabbit that had spoken first said.

'I want to go back.'

'You can't. We are all stuck here.'

'But I can't stay here,' I said in horror.

'Of course you can. Come with us. Mr Donut would love to see his creation.'

All I could do was to follow those creepy rabbits. All this was far beyond my brain's power to comprehend. After trying and failing to make sense of what was happening to me, I stopped.

Mr Donut was like a typical grandfather, only a little older, with a weird sense of fashion and the creepiest smile. He welcomed me like I was the winning lottery ticket.

'Hello, my dear,' he said in his sugary sweet voice.

'I want to go back,' I said, ignoring the hand he was offering me to shake.

He looked hurt by my words and suddenly I remembered my mom and her expression whenever I said something rude.

'But you've just come here,' he said, interrupting my thoughts. 'This place is so much better than your world.'

I remained quiet and he took my silence as a sign that I was listening. 'Tell me, were you really happy back home? Didn't you find life boring and repetitive? It was full of things you didn't want to face on a daily basis.'

His words caught my attention.

'What do you mean?' I asked.

'What I mean is that you should give this a try. My world is a happy place. Here there are no worries, no problems, no regrets,' he said softly, looking at me as if he was trying to read my thoughts. Maybe he really could. I *did* want to be in a place with no problems, no worries.

'No school, only fun, no studies; only parties and, the cherry on the pie, no pesky teachers.' It was enough to make me give in.

Mr Donut's world was great, no doubt. It had all the fun things a girl could dream of. I even came across a talking lion that was the colour of a peacock, a flying dolphin, mermaids, houses made of chocolates, diamonds, cakes and so many other things. Later I realized that the rabbits were the only normal creatures here. It was a whole new world for me.

I soon got a hang of how it all worked. Mr Donut dreamt something and the next day it was a part of his world. Mr Donut told me that dreaming up a human was very difficult for him for some unknown reason. I was the first one he was able to dream of who had her whole body intact and therefore, I was a treasure for him.

One thing he had said I could not forget. He had told me that there were things I wouldn't have to face here on a daily basis that I had to face back home. I always wondered about that. But whenever I tried to think about it, my head would start spinning. It seemed like something was meddling with my head, something that didn't want me to think of my own world. I couldn't ask anybody for help because these creatures were all thoughts—imaginary things that didn't have a past life to think about. And suddenly it all started feeling wrong.

One day, I marched into Mr Donut's lavish house and walked straight into his office, where he was standing in front of the window.

'What are you doing to me?' I asked him.

He turned and looked at me in confusion. 'What's wrong, dear?'

'You are doing something because I can't think straight. You're meddling with my brain,' I shouted.

'What's making you think so?' he asked in his sweet voice.

'Whenever I think of my home, my friends and about the life I used to have, I feel like I've lost them forever.'

'But you shouldn't even think of your past life. This place is so beautiful and your past life was a total waste.'

Suddenly I felt anger coursing through me and I shouted, 'NO! YOUR WORLD IS A TOTAL WASTE.'

The hurt on his face was heartbreaking and for a moment, it seemed like he was going to start crying. Immediately my thoughts drifted to my mother and I remembered all the times I had hurt her with my sharp words.

'Mr Donut,' I said softly. 'You have to understand. This world might be an escape from all the things I try to hide from every day but I don't want them gone forever. Maybe I *want* to have regrets and I *want* to make it up to all the people I have hurt. You can't keep me here. You have to send me back. Our life can be so much better if for once we stop being selfish and try to live for others instead of only for ourselves.'

Realization dawned on Mr Donut's face and he looked as if he had had an epiphany. He had been selfish. That was why he dreamt creatures into his world and controlled their lives. He needed enjoyment.

'Dear, don't you worry. You'll be back home tomorrow.'

I walked out of his house with excitement written clearly on my face. I saw Linda, one of the rabbits I had befriended.

'Linda, I'm going home.'

'You can't,' she said easily.

'But Mr Donut said so himself.'

Suddenly Linda became serious. 'Did he?'

'Yes.'

'Then maybe we are all going home,' she said quietly. 'The only way you can go back home is by destroying this dream world, and this world can only be destroyed if Mr Donut kills himself.' As she said these words, I felt myself spinning. Linda was gradually disappearing and I knew what was happening.

I sent out a silent prayer for Mr Donut and felt sad for what he did for me. Maybe he had made mistakes but I realized that he was a good man on the inside. My last thought as I felt myself drifting away was that I was going to miss the old man my whole life.

the tutor

Hiya Chowdhury, Age: 11, New Delhi

Annika was a genius...at everything except turning somersaults! She could remember all the rules of English grammar and all the laws of science. Her friends had to take tuitions, but not Annika. She could manage all by herself. But what a shock came her way when she reached the tenth standard and learnt that gymnastics would now be graded and there would be a somersaulting exam as well!

The whole house jumped through hoops for Annika. Even the furniture in the living room was shifted to give Annika room to practice! Agony for the guests, if you ask me. But when Annika saw her parents and brother somersault, she found that they were even worse at this than her. Annika grew tense. Now who would teach her to somersault? That night, her mother told her about an uncle who lived far away in Guwahati. He taught gymnastics in a school and was brilliant at turning somersaults. He seldom gave tuitions but her mother thought he might come to Delhi for Annika's sake. So next morning, a letter was sent to the uncle, telling him about the help required.

Annika kept checking her postbox everyday for a reply. A few days passed. Still there was nothing in the postbox. Then suddenly one day, Annika's uncle was at their doorstep. He wouldn't have fitted in the postbox anyway! He was a really short and sturdy man and his legs were very short too. He was ready in his gymnast's attire.

'Where do we start?' he asked in a squeak. Annika wanted to laugh. A short man in gym shorts and with a squeaky voice had come to teach her somersaults all the way from Guwahati!

Her uncle, however, was a very sincere tutor. He spent a lot of time teaching Annika the tricks of gymnastics. The family, too, helped. Every now and then her mother would bring him tea, her brother would bring him an energy drink and her father would ask him to try his disastrous pancakes! Slowly, Annika became friends with her tutor. Once over dinner, he told Annika that his only grief in life was that he was short. He told her that he used to teach sports in a school near his house but he did not like it. On being asked why, he said that all the children in his school made fun of him because he was short. When Annika's mother's letter reached him, he forgot the teasing, the sniggering and the jeering, and came to teach Annika.

Day after day passed and every day Annika learnt something new. She learnt how to use the back of her head while somersaulting. She even learnt how to walk on her hands! Then came the fateful day of the gymnastics examination. Annika was so nervous she could barely move. But when her turn finally came, she turned somersaults, walked on her hands and even turned cartwheels! After a few days, the results were announced. Annika had passed with flying colours! In fact, she had stood first in class in gymnastics!

That evening, she went to the bookshop and bought lots of books on gymnastics. She also bought a special book called *How To Grow Tall Without Much Exercise*. At night she quietly put the books in her tutor's suitcase in the hope that they would be of some use to him. With that, Annika went to sleep.

prelude to the mahabharata

Aatmik Gupta, Age: 13, New Delhi

The apsara android attempted to rouse Vishnu gently; she knew that he was being stubborn and was refusing to open his eyes on purpose. Growing exasperated, she declared, 'Wake up, paramdev! The council meeting is in fifteen minutes, and Brahma is not one to tolerate unpunctuality.'

Vishnu groaned and rose from the divan. 'Thank you, Shrutkirti. I'm sorry, I was just so tired. You can go now.'

He was truly grateful to her. In all the wildness of last night he had forgotten today's importance; he cursed himself for being so irresponsible. Today the entire council was meeting for the first time in the last three hundred years. It was only the third full meeting of the council since Swarg was founded a thousand years ago. Vishnu remembered the very first; it had been held in a different era altogether, when the surface of the moon was barren and undeveloped.

That had been a time of fear and despair. They had carried on their shoulders the immense guilt of causing the apocalypse, and there were only five hundred of them to bear that burden. It had been their extraordinary invention—the A.M.R.I.T. solution, over which the great nuclear war was fought. It killed 98 per cent of the world's population within a week, and condemned the rest to slowly perish from radiation poisoning.

In the meanwhile, the scientists escaped to the moon, using a massive shuttle prototype built by their leader, Brahma.

They had nothing with them but some equipment and a few vials of the A.M.R.I.T. solution. The latter they divided equally and drank. Then they set out on the laborious task of building a new world for themselves, cursing themselves each second for their role in the destruction of humanity.

Over the years, however, their guilt had eroded away. Their world had become so advanced and so luxurious that they no longer needed to trouble themselves with thoughts of their difficult beginnings. Their never-ending lives and immense intelligence allowed them to do whatever they pleased. Yet, Vishnu was always troubled by a question: could anything remain enjoyable for an eternity?

With that thought in his mind, Vishnu entered the teleporter.

◆

Vishnu walked down the large corridors of the administrative building, the grandest building in Swarg—a gigantic, perfectly symmetrical structure. The apsara android on duty escorted him to the centre of the building: the council hall, which was a vast, hollow sphere. The members of the council floated in as the gravitic lifts took them to their seats—magnetically floating pods that were arranged around the walls of the hall. The apsaras left, the doors shut, and a platform lifted a heavily bearded man into the centre of the hall.

Brahma's voice boomed across the hall. 'Council members, I know you are wondering why we have convened today. It is because we are faced with a serious problem. A few days ago, we sent a probe ship to Earth for the first time ever, and we discovered something stunning.'

He took a pause for effect.

'The probe found that the few survivors of the great war did not die out entirely. In fact, their population has expanded rapidly to almost a billion. And I do not talk about cave-men. They live in large, lead-lined, underground settlements where they are safe from radiation. And furthermore, they have recently started a space program.'

Excited chatter broke out in the assembly. Vishnu pressed the question button in his pod.

'Brahma, I just want to verify what you mean by your statements. You are implying that the humans may seek to attack us. Why would they do so?'

An attractive yet condescending voice spoke out. 'Well, if I may speak on behalf of President Brahma: it is obvious. They would seek to avenge the destruction of Earth.' It was Indra.

'And you have proof of this?'

Brahma hesitated and then spoke. 'Not exactly. The probe ship tells us that the new humans actually consider us to be Gods.'

Saraswati broke in. 'And you expect them to attack *us*, the beings they revere the most?'

Indra replied, 'But they could certainly prove to be a threat in the future. I do not propose we attack them outright, only manipulate them to ensure they remain harmless. After all, we must do everything we can to protect Swarg. Those who agree with me, flash your pods green.'

It became evident that the majority of the council agreed with Indra.

Brahma began to speak, but Vishnu cut in sharply. 'You have all voted wrongly. Instead of embracing that wondrous world we lost a millennium ago, you are scared of it. Scared of its people. You no longer care about humanity because you do not consider yourself a part of it any more. You forget that we are humans ourselves. I cannot agree with you any longer. I cannot remain a Swargvasi any longer. Goodbye. I am leaving for Earth.'

Vishnu ignored the stunned silence that followed his pronouncement. He teleported directly to the aerodrome. Entering his shuttle, he keyed in Earth as his destination. Then he asked the computer to alter his image to fit an alias. The computer drew up a list of identities to choose from. He liked the last one.

'Selected: Krishna avatar. Confirm?' the computer asked.

'Yes.'

Krishna reached Earth and soon set in motion the cycle of events which would culminate in the Mahabharata.

guardians

Dipali Lath, Age: 13, Hyderabad

It was another typical morning at home. I woke up to the strangely synchronized yelling of my brother, mother and father. Funnily enough, all their yells were directed at me.

'Why did you use my computer yesterday without asking me?' hollered my brother, when I *had* actually asked his permission. (He really behaves like an amnesiac sometimes.)

'Why did you leave the newspaper spread out all over the dining table?' came from my mother, when I hadn't even read the paper yet.

'How come you're still sleeping?' was my father's question, which didn't make any sense, since it was practically impossible for anyone to remain asleep amidst the cacophony of shrieks.

Once I had irately answered them all, I stumbled through brushing my teeth, taking a shower, eating breakfast, and doing what every student typically does before leaving for school. Even these everyday tasks were torturous; because alongside them I had to fight with my brother to use the washroom first, argue with my mother about my birthday gift and debate with my father about changing my school. All in all, just another typical morning at home.

As it turned out, school was just as amazing that day. My two best friends, Anandita and Preeti, chose to ignore me the whole day because I had forgotten to bring some material for our group project (apparently the entire reason why Ma'am had given a 'B+' instead of an 'A'). Of course, they overlooked the fact that neither of them had got *their* stuff either. But hey, I was the one who had forgotten the oh-so-important sketch pens! I usually don't mind their silliness, but since I was already having a bad day, I decided to take a break from their unreasonably cold stares and furious whispering during the ride back home.

By the time I boarded the bus, they had found themselves a seat for two, and were obviously expecting me to beg them to shift back to our old seat, where we could all squeeze in together like a human sandwich. To their utmost surprise, and mine too in fact, I confidently strode over to an empty seat in the back. I dumped my bag there and sat down. Even though I had an excellent poker face on, it didn't change the fact that I was feeling lonely without my two eccentric companions.

I was hoping I would get to sit alone and wallow in my loneliness, but it was a futile hope. The new girl, Suchitra, ended up sitting beside me, much to the satisfaction of my dear friends. Their smirks drove me to the point of initiating a conversation with her, and voila, I surprised myself for the second time that day. At first she was a little reclusive, but soon she was animatedly chatting with me about markets, celebrities and comics. It was as though we had known each other for years!

While chatting, I suddenly blurted out, 'Doesn't your family constantly nag you about the littlest of things? I mean, sure, I love my family, but don't they sometimes get on your nerves? And friends too. Sometimes I wish they weren't so... dramatic, you know?' She nodded understandingly, then added with a wink, 'But what's life without a little bit of drama?' I smiled at her reply, shrugged, and we continued our conversation.

After we had run out of things to talk about, an awkward silence hung between us. Meanwhile, my friends' bus stop had arrived. They couldn't resist giving me one more scornful look before stepping down, at which I rolled my eyes theatrically. Suchitra noticed and burst out laughing, causing me to erupt in laughter too. It was a pleasant sound, one that lasted for a while.

Soon, her stop arrived. After we wished each other the customary goodbye she paused and told me, 'You're really nice, you know? And, um, I know this sounds a bit weird, but still, you're lucky to have the kind of family and friends you have. I think you should forgive them for the nagging and stuff, and just, um...hold on to them, I guess.' She said this hurriedly. By the time I could comprehend what she had said, she was on the pavement. While we waved to each other, my grey cells tried to decipher why she had told me such a thing.

As my stop drew near, I pushed it out of my mind, assuring myself that there was no particular reason behind it, and that she was probably just trying to make me feel better. Instead, I wondered how I could convince my mother to buy me a new camera—something I had been longing for since months (yes, my birthday gift).

If only I had looked back, I would have been able to understand the true worth of Suchitra's words. If only I had turned around, I would have noticed that she had turned away from the row of neat, independent houses around her stop and was instead walking towards a tall brick building. On it hung the sign: 'THE GUARDIAN ORPHANAGE'.

a home for genie

Gifty Prabhas, Age: 15, Kurnool

The cacophony of honking vehicles filled the streets of Gandhi Nagar like it did every working day. Mr Ajay Singh's house, easily recognizable from the main street, was a little less chaotic that Monday morning. And the reason was his sickness. He had even taken leave from his office, which was most unlike him. He was a hard-working man who never took a holiday. However his son, Jeetender, though not sick, had declared a school holiday for himself after pretending to have a headache and fooling his mother. Ajay's daughter, the even naughtier younger child, did not feel good about going to school leaving her brother and father untroubled at home.

Ajay Singh's house that day was surprisingly pleasant. No one, including Mrs Singh, uttered a word as they sat at the large dining table, inherited from Ajay Singh's mother, and ate the hearty Punjabi breakfast. As soon as they finished, everyone departed to their rooms without quarrelling, laughing, singing—in fact without doing anything that would result in a sound. Surely, that morning was different from others.

Mrs Singh got busy making phone calls, talking to her old friends, relatives and former neighbours, ringing them up and troubling them, one after the other. Jeetender relaxed by listening to music. Ajay Singh could only stare at the street, hoping for the noise to end so that he could finish his crime thriller in peace.

So the day passed. Everyone felt bad for taking leave and hoped for the day to end soon. But time never acts the way you want it to. There were still a few hours till night fell and the moon appeared. Mrs Singh was busy in the kitchen preparing dinner and singing songs as always. When she was about to cook the rice and start another song, she heard a knock on the door. Usually, Ajay Singh got annoyed if visitors dropped by unannounced, but that day he was so bored that as soon as he heard the knock, he rushed to the door to find who was there. He reached the door faster than his wife, but allowed her to open the door. He didn't want to be seen in his pyjamas. Mrs Singh spoke to someone, but her husband was not able to figure out who it was. By now he was curious enough to appear at the door. But he was met with severe disappointment for there was only a poor lamp seller at the door. Who bought lamps these days, or even used them? No one in Gandhi Nagar; no one in the whole of Delhi. Lamps were only traces of the past, to be preserved, but definitely not to be used or bought and sold in the capital city. If it was any other day, Ajay Singh would have closed the door the moment he saw a person selling lamps on his doorstep but today he needed to have a conversation, so he started talking to the man. From his appearance, it was clear that the lamp seller was poorer than the poor. He had been begging people to buy his lamps on the streets but everyone had dismissed him by saying, 'Who wants this junk?' Ajay Singh was the only one to stop and speak to him.

Ajay Singh *did* buy a lamp, which the lamp seller handed over to him with trembling hands. He was not interested in using the lamp but the beauty of the golden-coloured piece attracted him so much that he took it. His daughter, seeing

BLAH
BLAH
BLA
BLEBLAHH
BLA
BLA
BLAH
BLAH
BLAH
PEEEEEEEE
POM
PA
BEEP BEEP

it in her father's hand, asked childishly, 'Is that Aladin's lamp?' (It really wasn't that childish given what happened next.) Her father replied, just to add some excitement to his day, 'Yes it is. You want it?'

'YES!' she answered, her eyes shining with excitement. Ajay Singh began waving the lamp over his head to tease his daughter and she jumped excitedly to reach the lamp. And in his attempts to tease her and in her attempts to take hold of it, Ajay Singh lost his grip. The lamp fell with a thud on the floor.

'Papaaaaaaa! What did you do! See, now the genie will come out!' she shouted, half-afraid and half-excited. Ajay Singh opened his mouth to let out a laugh, but instead a shocked yell came from it. There was a genie standing right in front of his eyes. He yelled once again and louder, just to make sure it wasn't a dream. He stood still in utter disbelief and horror. Sometimes when adults are frozen in fear, children know just what to do or say. His daughter did not panic in the least. Ajay Singh's yell had brought his son and wife running to the room as well. When they reached him, there were two other shocked yells and Mrs Singh fainted. Jeetender were so terrified that they couldn't move an inch. It was only the naughty little girl who came forward and spoke. 'Who are you?' she asked. The genie replied in its thundering yet pleasing voice, 'I am Genie.'

What happened next? Mr and Mrs Singh and their son soon recovered from the shock and started smiling. This genie was an old and experienced genie and did not grant wishes blindly. It granted only those wishes that gave the family peace and happiness. Now, there was no more quarrelling in the house. They were happy to be in each other's company without being bored. Even the cacophony on the busy streets of Gandhi Nagar did not bother them! In fact, after a while, they seldom asked Genie for wishes and it grew fat without any work. After all, what more does a family require other than happiness, love and understanding?

the upside-downy

Krutika Pandya, Age: 10, Aurangabad

I've always wished that the world would turn upside down. That happened on 9 October 2011.

Uncle Fred came to visit us from New York. He was a great inventor. He had made his latest invention, which he called the Upside-Downy. He gave me a demo. He told me, 'Just stay in the house and I will be in my secret HQ.' Then he whispered to me, 'HQ is my underground workshop. I'll stay there so it doesn't affect me.'

1, 2, 3, 4, 5...

Uncle Fred pushed the blue button and with a tremendous jerk, the world turned upside down. In the next couple of seconds, I found myself on my soft bed.

When I woke up after the best sleep ever, I realized that I had to do everything upside down. I had to brush my teeth standing on my head and I had to do almost everything else on my head.

On Sunday I had my gymnastics championship which I generally hate. But this time I was pretty excited because I had been selected for balancing on my head. I was an expert in that by now. But I practised some more anyway.

So came the big day. There were lots of participants but no one was better than me. And as everyone knew I was going to win, they didn't even dare to cheer for anyone else. My friend Jerry had also come with his dad, who was the owner of an ice cream company. He had brought his lovely

ice cream van. Then the competition started. I was about to win but the ice cream distracted me and I lost.

I was extremely sad because I had been overconfident. I couldn't take it anymore, so that same day I went to Uncle Fred's HQ. The underground lift was stuck so I had to dig through the moist soil while standing on my head. It was the toughest challenge of my life. But I didn't have a choice. Finally, I managed.

I went to Uncle Fred with tears flowing down my cheeks. I mumbled in an upset voice, 'Make everything go back to normal because firstly, I've got a bad headache from standing on my head all the time and secondly, I can't live like this.'

So Uncle Fred said, 'All right, I'll change everything back to normal.'

6, 7, 8, 9, 10…

He pushed the purple button and everything went back to normal. Everything was back just the way it always was.

our champa tree

Chandra Mohaan Roy, Age: 15, Kolkata

The other day, while I was reading the poem 'Our Casuarina Tree' by Toru Dutt, my mind flew back to the golden days of my childhood. We had a tree—a champa tree—the variety we call Golon champa. This tree was situated just in front of the entrance to our house, behind the main gate, and nearly touched the boundary wall of our neighbour's house. It was magnificent and used to bear white flowers with a golden tinge at the centre and had broad green leaves. It was quite tall, nearly reaching the top of our century-old three-storied house. I had seen this tree from the time I was born, and it was like an old friend. It was planted by my grandpa when he was a child, probably about seventy-five years ago.

A few months after my grandpa passed away, I was deeply shocked to hear that the tree was going to be uprooted. Its roots had cracked the water pipelines of our neighbour's house. My mom also pointed out several other problems—the tree spoiled the view of the entrance to our house; the dried leaves and flowers clogged the drain; the droppings of the birds perching on the tree were a constant menace. I vehemently pleaded with them to save the tree, but all my arguments were futile. At last, Mom grew impatient and angrily shouted at me, 'If our neighbours demand compensation because of the damage caused, will you be able to foot the bill?' So finally the line was drawn.

Every season was special to me because of this tree. In the

sultry months of summer, I fervently waited to see its top sway and dance madly to the wild tune of the thunderstorms. The pitter-patter sound of the first raindrops falling on the leaves indicated the advent of monsoon. As winter approached, the leaves withered and their rustling sound rung in my ears. During spring, the tree would be covered with those wonderful flowers and tiny green leaf buds. In the morning, the lane would be strewn with freshly fallen flowers—really an incredible sight. I felt that my friend had shed its old leaves and had attired itself in an entirely new look—just the way I would be ready for the next academic year with a new uniform.

Perhaps this tree kindled my love for nature. During lonely summer afternoons, when everyone was busy at work, I used to gaze at the tree and watch the crows cawing loudly on the branches, the mynahs fighting and the sparrows twittering. It was truly bliss to observe nature so closely. With the tree gone, I would miss the chirping of the birds, the cool breeze in the mornings, those beautiful flowers and would also lose a very good friend. But above all, this tree was a glowing reminiscence of my grandfather and of those playful days of childhood.

On the fateful day it was cut down, I could not control myself. Hot tears swelled up in my eyes and then rolled down my cheeks endlessly as I watched the branches being chopped off mercilessly. I was shocked by man's might. A tree took nearly seventy-five years to reach that height, but men took only three hours to demolish it! Then those marauders, with all their strength, started to uproot its trunk. No matter how hard they hit, the tree, with its brown strong roots, clung firmly to the soil as if holding on with clenched fists. They finally had to quit as the roots of the tree ran very deep. I knew then that no one could uproot this tree, neither from my heart, nor from this soil. I heaved a sigh of relief; at least this stump would remind me of the splendid tree.

But I was robbed forever of the company of my childhood friend. The birds never came back on their much frequented sojourn; the green foliage vanished in this concrete jungle. My mom consoled me that within a few months, the tree would start to grow once again. But a year passed and there was no sign of it. I gently stroked its rough stump every day, trying to soothe its pain and my eyes frantically searched for even a small green bud. Alas, to no avail. The light brown stump slowly turned into a deep black colour. I got accustomed to its absence and lost all hope. I learnt a great lesson—that the world hardly cares to look back at foolish childish sentiments. My soul cried out:

'That would thy beauty fain, oh, fain rehearse,
May Love defend thee from Oblivion's curse.'

Then yesterday, while returning from school, suddenly I noticed that a small sprout had appeared on the champa tree. My heart leapt with joy. It was not over yet. A new saga would begin all over again. Will this twig pave the way for another magnificent tree? I was euphoric at first but immediately a deep fear haunted me—will they uproot it fully now? No, I have a strong hunch that this little twig will be able to regain the past grandeur of my beloved champa tree.

hunting acorns at sanjay malhotra laboratories

Manaal Jahan, Age: 12, Bangalore

When Diya reached home from school, she immediately went to her room. She sat down at her table and started doing Physics sums. Finding a sum difficult, she looked out of the window, trying to work out the answer. There she saw a squirrel tapping away with an acorn. 'The answer is $E=mc^2$' came a soft squeak. Diya was very surprised. She thought to herself, 'I must have remembered the answer, and thought it was coming from that little creature. We must be telepathetic!' A squeaky voice came from outside the window: 'It's not telepathetic! The word you're looking for is telepathic! Gosh, you're not very smart, are you?'

Diya jumped up from her chair with an astonished expression on her face. She asked softly, 'What are you?' The squirrel replied tartly. 'Firstly, I'm not a what, I'm a who! I'm Furry, from Sanjay Malhotra Laboratories. Will you please help me?' Stunned, Diya just nodded. 'Thank you,' Furry said. 'Now, let me explain. In Sanjay Malhotra Laboratories, there are many animals being tested on by inserting other genes into them. Well, accidentally, Mr Malhotra's genes were inserted into me. In return, my genes went to him. I panicked and transferred his genes to all the other animals there. But it can be reversed. That is where you come in. I feel very bad for Mr Malhotra, who is now always gnawing on an acorn as his family watches him pitifully. I need you to come and reverse it!'

Diya said 'All right, I'll help you. Come at night and knock on my window. Then you can lead to me to the lab.'

That night, Diya hurriedly finished her dinner and ran upstairs to her room. There, she found Furry knocking furiously on her window. He squeaked, 'Let's go!' And off they went to the laboratory.

Inside the laboratory, Furry introduced Diya to all the other animals. There were Horis and Doris, the mice, Hardy, the beaver and Terra, the old and wise turtle.

Furry directed Diya to the machine that had caused all the damage. It was white, and had many coloured buttons on it. 'Which one is the reverse button?' Diya asked. Horis and Doris started jumping up and down and shouting, 'Press the red button!' At that Mr Malhotra squeaked loudly from his chair! Furry translated, 'He's saying "You fools! Do you want us all to die? The red button will destroy the entire laboratory!"' Hardy said, 'I know! It's the yellow button!' Mr Malhotra started running in circles and squeaked loudly. Furry said, 'He means to say "No! No! The yellow button will self-destruct the machine and we will be stuck like this forever!"' Diya went to Mr Malhotra and asked, 'Sir, which is the reverse button? Surely, you must know.' Mr Malhotra was silent for a while, and then squeaked very softly. Furry said, 'He means "There are so many buttons; I forgot which one does what!"' There was silence in the lab. Finally Diya said, 'I'm sorry. I tried to help you. I am very sorry!' Terra, who rarely spoke, said softly, 'Diya, dear, come over here. The button you must press is the colour of a bean. The most important button is green!'

As Diya pressed the green button, all the animals started running helter-skelter. One mouse slipped and fell on a few buttons, pressing them as he went. The machine blew up and smoke started rising from it. Once the smoke cleared, all the animals found that they were themselves again. Furry and Mr Malhotra turned to thank Diya, but couldn't find her anywhere. 'Diya? Where are you? Diya?'

A loud squeak made them look down, where they found Diya on all fours, scrambling behind an acorn...

monsters vs aliens

Vipul Vaibhav, Age: 15, Varanasi

Ever heard of a virtual world?

Yeah, I was in one! How does it feel when you suddenly wake up to find that your bed, your room, everything, has just disappeared and you are in a void? Trust me, it feels horrible.

I was sitting in the void. It was dark. The only source of light was coming from the other end and I calculated that it was far…very far.

Suddenly, the ground rumbled. I got up, ready to run. But my legs felt like they were frozen. Maybe with fear. I pushed myself forward but I couldn't move an inch.

The ground rumbled again. My heart pounded fast, ready to burst out of my ribs. I was numb with fear. Things became blurry. I was sure I saw something in the light. Then I passed out.

◆

I woke up with a start. I looked around me. It was not the same void I had woken up in last time. This was different. This was a void, yes, but it was illuminated and I could see decorations hanging on the wall.

Was that a teeth, tied with a string? Yes, it was. I looked at myself. I was dressed as a clown and tied up. Thin golden threads were holding me down.

It took me some strength but I broke free from them.

The bed I was sitting on was covered with pictures of strange animals. I decided to take a look around. I put my feet down but they didn't hit anything solid. I frowned and looked down.

What I saw took away my breath. My bed was suspended in air and below me there was...nothing. (Of course, I reminded myself, it was a void after all.) My eyes fell upon some stones suspended in the void.

It might be a path, I thought.

So I carefully stepped on them praying that they would take my weight. Luckily it was no different from walking on a stone path. I jumped from one stone to the other till I saw a door.

I had never been so happy to see a door before.

I jumped from stone to stone faster now. Suddenly, my right foot slipped and I was about to fall, but I caught the stone just in time. I pulled myself up and this time, I cautiously stepped on the remaining stones. When I reached the door, I was exhausted. I was panting and covered in sweat.

I turned the knob and flung the door open.

It was very bright on the other side. My eyes took time to adjust to the brightness. When I opened my eyes after a few seconds, a big—very big—meadow lay in front of me. At first I thought it was deserted but then I saw it...

If you think that all monsters are humongous then please discard the thought. In front of me were hundreds of tiny monsters (if you say that I shouldn't call them monsters then let me correct you). Those beasts were like platypuses but the difference was that they had horns on their heads, many of them were multicoloured and they all had very sharp claws.

As they noticed me, they squeaked. Everyone looked up and then, to my amazement, in a fraction of a second, I saw

all of them circling around me.

I was scared. I wanted to step on those monsters and run away but their sheer number stopped me.

I could hear them murmuring to each other. Then one of them looked at me and spoke (yes, you read it right, they *spoke*). It sounded like, 'Akjab Mahady Khws?'

I stared at the monster. The monster stared back at me. I looked around. All the monsters had their eyes fixed on me.

Suddenly one of them came to the one who had spoken to me and whispered something in his ear. The first one considered whatever the second had said to him and then he turned around and farted. (Yeah, farted. Please stop smirking, I hate that!) The air was filled with a blue gas that almost choked me. After a while, I recovered. The monster now repeated his question. This time, I understood him.

'Who are you?' His voice surprised me. It was deep and strict.

'Er...I am...' (Hey, had I introduced myself? Oops, sorry, completely forgot about that!) 'I am Jason Bourne. Thirteen years old. I am from New York.'

Perhaps I had spoken too much because at the words 'New York', those things panicked. Many of them screamed while others gravely spoke to each other.

The one who had spoken to me remained calm. 'What brings you here?'

I scratched my head. I couldn't recall how I came here. Where was I before I woke up in that dark void?

'Er, I don't know. But where am I?' I asked, trying to sound confident.

'Monsterin town, of course!' he replied in a matter-of-fact tone. 'Anyway, I am Nexus.'

'Cool name!' I gave him a weak smile.

Suddenly Nexus came near me and smelled me. His eyes widened.

'You,' he grumbled. 'You are an ALIEN.' He sounded offended. At the same time, all the other tiny beasts snarled at me.

'Wait! What do you mean, ALIEN? I am a human!' I tried to explain in vain.

Then, to my horror, those beasts stood on their hind legs and summoned their staffs. Out of nowhere, long sticks turned up in their hands. Each stick had a face just like its owner's drawn on it.

I was left with no other choice than to run for my life. I think I did squash some of the monsters but I had no other thought in my mind than running.

They shouted while I ran. One said, 'You can never rescue them, Alien!' Another said, 'We'll call our big brothers for help and they'll tear you all to pieces!'

Suddenly a giant vulture came, grabbed me and flew off with me. The monsters pointed jets of rays from their staffs at me but the vulture was clever. She flew in a zigzag manner so that the monsters couldn't get a good shot.

My good sense told me to stay still in the claws of the giant vulture. The vulture had now left the monsters and was flying to a big mountain. I told myself to get ready to become a meal for this giant bird of prey. But as the vulture flew nearer the mountain, I saw something moving. I sighed in relief. Almost fifty other humans were standing at the edge of the cliff.

The vulture released me on the cliff just a few feet above the ground. I fell down hard and almost rolled off the edge of the cliff. The other humans saved me just in time.

Everyone cheered as I got to my feet. They were all normal humans but their clothes were tattered and the men all had long beards.

'Um…hi,' I said. Everyone cheered again. Many of them came and touched my feet.

'At last you are here, lord of the aliens!' one of them cried.

'What are you talking about? I am no lord.' I was alarmed.

Everyone cheered again.

'Please stay silent everyone,' I shouted. 'Give me an explanation!'

One man came to me. 'My lord, maybe you are not aware of the prophecy.' He produced a scroll and handed it to me.

The scroll was very very old. I opened it. It read:

'The son of a man,
has the power that he can
protect everyone from monsters
and bring home peace and lobsters.
Vulture shall be his ride,
And he shall help you fight.
Modest shall be he,
And help you be free.'

I looked up. 'Lobsters?'

'Yes, my lord. They are good luck charms for peace and they also defend us,' the man spoke.

'Where do you find them?' I asked.

They smiled. 'Ah! That is the quest, my lord. We have to fight the monsters and restore the lobsters so that we can be free.'

'Won't any normal lobster work?' I asked hopefully.

'No, my lord. Only the golden lobster is the talisman that can teleport us home,' was the reply.

I was too tired to ask any more questions. 'So we can start tomorrow.'

Everyone cheered again.

The man who had told me everything said, 'My lord, I shall show you your stone.'

'Stone?'

He guided me to a stone which was like a bed.

I sat down and he started telling me everything, how he had discovered himself here, how he had seen others come here too, how they had been waiting for the prophecy to come true.

'The monsters were always our enemies.'

'So why are we called aliens?' I asked.

He smiled. 'Don't you realize, my lord? We are on a magical asteroid.'

◆

The sun was shining overhead when we started the journey. The man who had told me everything, who called himself Ma'lakh, guided us.

'When I first came here,' he told me, 'I came on this very path, that's why I remember the way.'

I smiled.

On the way Ma'lakh taught everyone how to fight the monsters.

'The monsters are not very strong but they have staffs. Those are their only weapons. The best way to fight them is to tickle them on their noses and they'll disintegrate. That is their punishment, as far as I recall.'

So all I had to do was tickle them on their noses? Sounded easy, didn't it?

But it wasn't easy at all. When after crossing two deadly rivers and five freezing mountains, we reached the border of the land of monsters, we were totally exhausted.

Ma'lakh shouted, 'Give us the lobster and we shall spare you.'

Then I saw those filthy monsters again. Anger swelled up inside me. We all charged with feathers in our hand (which we had already arranged for).

The monsters injured many of us with their spells. But we managed to reduce many of them to dust.

One of them shot me in the chest and I was flung far away. That was when I saw it.

A shining golden statue kept on a table.

No monster was paying attention to me so I ran for the statue. When they finally noticed me near the statue they screamed and shot many spells at me but they were too late. I already had the statue in my hand and its aura surrounded me.

I heard a whisper in my ears. 'You were worthy so you got this.'

I ran towards the battlefield and felt an invisible force helping me tickle away those nasty monsters.

When the monsters saw that there were only a few of them left they fled for their lives while the humans cheered.

'We have done well, my lord. Now we shall go back to our lovely earth,' Ma'lakh said.

I realized I didn't know how to go back. I wondered how these humans would feel when they found out. But again I heard a voice in my head, 'Do not worry. Put this statue, I mean me, down and speak these three magical words…'

I did as I was told. I put the statue down and spoke the three magical words while holding everyone's hands. 'Akamaka Shadeis Earth.' Suddenly the place dissolved.

◆

When I opened my eyes, I was lying on a bed again but thankfully, this time it was my own. I sat up and saw my mother's concerned eyes.

'How do you feel now, dear?' she asked.

'Good. What had happened to me?' I was confused.

'Oh! You were suffering from high fever, so I made you sleep.'

I gaped at her. 'So it was just a dream?' I asked myself.

And, to my horror, came a reply, 'No dear, it was all real. All you were doing was fighting the pathogens in your body.'

Then my mother added, 'If you feel better you should complete...'

Even before she completed her sentence it hit me. I had to submit a story for a competition called Young Authors Hunt.

'Sure Mom!' I jumped off my bed. 'I have got the best story of my life!'

And I started typing the story.

the book of mysteries

Siddharth Golwalkar, Age: 9, Noida

One morning, I woke up and found a parcel lying at my doorstep. I picked it up and saw it was from my Aunt Sally the Third. There was nothing in it but a card. Behind the card was a treasure map. On seeing the map I almost jumped out of my pants. Holy moly! I love treasure hunts!

I could not wait. I took a cab and went to the airport. I boarded a flight to Mexico. When I arrived at Mexico City, I could hear people talking in Spanish but the problem was that I didn't understand Spanish. I wished I had completed school before jumping into this treasure hunting thing. But I knew I had to get going. So I boarded a ship to Haiti and from there, I took a helicopter to the treasure island. On the way, a storm came and our helicopter's engine failed. Down I went and bingo! I landed on the treasure island. I slept on the beach.

The next day, before I got up, a bird pooped on my head. How shameful! While I was walking I felt the earth tremble underneath me. A tsunami! I ran like the go-karts that I had seen on television. While running, I fell into a deep hole. I landed on a plain surface and walked for about a kilometre. I came to a deep gorge and across the gorge was a door. So I took courage and stepped into the gorge. Mama mia! My foot fell on a magnetic rock and by stepping on the rocks I carefully crossed the gorge. I opened the door, and guess what, the room was filled with gold. Right in the centre of

START HERE
HOLY MOLY!
TAXI!
ZZZZZZZ
OOPS!
YUM! MIRINDA!
HMM...
SOS

QUE PASA!!
??
HAITI
TREASURE ISLAND
KA-BOOM!
A MiA!
THIS IS PARADISE!
BOOK OF MYST-ERIES
HOME

the room was a book. On it was written: *The Book of Mysteries.*

I took the book and turned back. Just when I took a step, I fell down and a gold treasure map fell out. How weird. I followed the treasure map that led me out. Outside, I saw that most of the island had been washed away by the tsunami. The map led me to a volcano. There was a sign that said that whoever is courageous will jump into the volcano. While I was wondering what to do, something pushed me from behind and I fell into the volcano. I got ready to be burnt by hot lava. But it was not lava! It was Mirinda soda. How odd. I also found that now when I jumped I could jump fifty times higher because of magma force. I took a high jump that took me out of the volcano.

When I came out I felt dizzy. I should have helped myself to a little of that Mirinda, I thought. Never mind. There was no way I was going back to such a place again. It was time to go home so I went to the beach and sent out an SOS signal. A rescue boat came to take me back to Mexico but before that I asked them to take out all the gold from the cave. I distributed the gold among the Mexicans and took a flight back home. What a trip that was!

the world beneath us

Anjali Bhavan, Age: 14, New Delhi

I was sitting in the school playground, bunking classes as usual. As I pulled the braid of Ishita, my best friend, I couldn't help wondering if life could be just a bit different.

All of a sudden, I heard something creak below the bench I was sitting on (yes, our school has benches in the playground, as if it's a park for hunchbacked oldies to stroll and chew betel nuts). Surprised, I bent down, and saw the grass under my feet move. Ishita and I got down on our knees and started digging.

And lo and behold, there was a tunnel!

Both of us descended into it. I helped Ishita down first. After I entered the tunnel, I covered the opening above us with my big art file, so that no one could come down after us.

We went down and down, until at last we entered a wide space, which seemed amazingly serene. There were people there—but there was nothing special about them. There were roads, buildings, parks, everything, and it seemed as if Ishita and I had just entered another city.

Except the roads here were spotlessly clean, the people incredibly quiet, and the buildings small, nearly all of the same type, and coloured in simple tones.

'Wow…' Ishita whispered, as we began walking down a street. 'This is so…*Alice in Wonderland!*'

'But the people are humans here,' I reminded her.

We kept on walking, and noticed that there were no

automobiles anywhere. In fact, people were either walking, riding on a horse, or riding chariots! And what was more, they were all dressed in ancient Indian clothing—those robes worn by men and women of yore. No commotion, no traffic—it was as if we had gone back a thousand years!

We stopped a man. 'Excuse me, what place is this?' we asked. 'And kindly forgive our cheekiness, but who are you all?'

The man stared at both of us for a brief while. Of course we looked like outsiders in our uniform!

'You are in Mohenjo-daro,' the man answered.

Ishita stared at him, thinking he was nuts. 'Excuse me, we are in the year 2013...'

'What?'

'Uh, sorry...' I answered, silencing Ishita with my gaze.

'This is Mohenjo-daro, the capital city of Indutva, our country,' the man explained.

'Then...then this is the valley of the Indus?'

'The civilization of the valley of the Indus, but not the location,' the man replied. 'We moved out of that place when it became a desert due to the advancement of technology and environmental degradation. The world began believing that we had been wiped out, but we had just moved underground—literally.'

'How old are you?' Ishita asked suspiciously. 'You aren't immortal or anything, right?'

'Of course not!' The man threw back his head and laughed. 'I am around forty. You seem new here.'

'Oh yes. We stumbled on to this place accidentally,' I said. 'So...you must have a king?'

'Of course! I'll take you to him.'

We met the king, a muscular youth, quite unlike the potbellied, moustached kings we usually saw in cartoon shows and plays. He looked around twenty-five years old.

'You can stay here for today,' the king, whose name was Suryadhwaj, said to us after the introductions were done. 'Right here in the palace.'

I stared at Ishita.

What about our parents? Our school?

'We would like to talk about this in private, Your Highness,' Ishita bowed. 'Are we granted permission?'

The king liked Ishita's quiet, polite demeanour. 'Of course.'

'Damn! Our parents!' Ishita whispered hoarsely. 'We might be graduating from school next week, but that doesn't make us old enough to live without our parents!'

'Relax,' I advised her. 'We'll stay here. Who is going to know? We can return before dispersal—you have your watch, don't you?'

◆

Since school had just begun when we had come down to Indutva, we had a leisurely seven hours at our disposal to explore the capital city. We went around with gusto, despite not knowing the directions. The courteous citizens were more than happy to help. We changed into the attire of the Indutvans, provided to us by the king's younger sister, who was the same age as us.

We noticed that everyone talked in low tones here; and people had perfect control over their anger and emotions. The only extreme emotion they showed was a burst of laughter. Everything was kept spotlessly clean and there were no poor people begging on the streets. The greenery we saw in that one city would not be found in the whole of Rajasthan, I dare say. (Rajasthan is where we both live, by the way.)

In no time, we fell in love with the city. It was a far

cry from bustling, dirty Jaipur, and ironically, we, who were notorious in school for rebellion, found ourselves longing to live here, in this land of perfect order.

There were no problems of irrigation, agriculture or anything else. Everything was provided for here, and water was brought by a canal dug from the Indus and distributed through special channels designed by expert engineers.

Here, kings didn't become kings on the basis of heredity. Aspiring kings had to take rigorous tests, not just written, but other tests like swordfighting (yes, they still had swordfighting), politics, their ability to connect with people. All this was told to us by the guide Suryadhwaj, who was sent with us.

When Ishita's watch showed 1:30 p.m., we realized it was time to go; school would be closing ten minutes from now.

Then we realized something: that the peace eluding us in the eighteen years of our existence in Jaipur—the dream and hope of a simple, uncomplicated life full of goodness—was right before us. Could we leave it all for the bustle of Jaipur? Who knew if Indutva would survive until we made up our minds to return?

And shouldn't we be fighting to establish the Indutva way of living?

Ishita and I stared at each other and took each other's hand.

We're living here, we thought.

◆

Twelve years have passed. Ishita and I are still good friends and are going strong at thirty. Ishita fell in love with Suryadhwaj and married him, while I am still unmarried. Here, life is much better than what I could have ever dreamt of. We work hard for our living, have eased our rebellious spirit with our increasing maturity, and are at peace.

I have learnt swordfighting, while Ishita is now an expert archer. I have quite a lot of friends now, including the man we had first met, who's now fifty-two.

Our parents never found us. We once went up and secretly peeked into our old homes: our parents were not yet reconciled to our disappearance, which broke our hearts.

But we could not return. Indutva was now our land, and we could never think of leaving it. It was this place that had taught us the true value of love, kindness, compassion, courage and courtesy. We have realized that there can be a whole new world beyond Facebook, online chats, McDonald's and fighting for notebooks. It may not necessarily be a secret land like Indutva, but it *can* be a world of goodness and peace. It all depends on how you want your world to be, and how you allow your fate to guide you.

the speaking tree

Kaavyayani Pal, Age: 12, Gurgaon

It may be hard to believe, but once upon a time I was a mere result of a science project.

The children planted me in a plastic cup full of damp cotton. Ah! It was such a luxury, with no worms to gnaw on my roots and no insects to burden my arms. The children often fought over chances to water me, and the teachers praised my growth. In other words, I was spoilt.

There was nothing that could shock a spoilt sapling more than being given away. I was appalled when a lady snatched me away from my haven in the classroom and deposited me in her garden. I was devastated. Nobody ever visited me except a grumpy gardener who watered me once a day. The other trees and plants would not talk to me, and for a while, I thought that they were ganging up on me. I was still young and my view was blocked by a peach tree in front of me. I missed my perch on the class windowsill.

Then one day, a disaster occurred. The house to which the garden belonged caught fire. Thankfully, I was not in the danger zone, but the heat still seared me. I had never imagined such heat and brightness; it was as though the sun had been brought down right on top of me. I was frightened.

Luckily, I was not hurt much, but the other plants were. For the first time, I stopped thinking of myself, and instead thought of others. I tipped my leaves so they could quench the ground's thirst with dew. I stopped wilting and grew strong and tall, much to the gardener's joy. My foliage hung over the garden and my fruits—mangoes—brought the lady wealth. I became caring.

But my trial was far from over. Along with wealth, my mangoes also attracted strange visitors—some needed, some unwanted. In the latter group was the woodcutter.

Even when he sauntered in that evening, his axe hanging loosely by his side, I knew he was not to be trusted. His eyes glittered a mean shade of yellow and his teeth shone the same colour. He limped on his left leg, but the oversized brown boots made it impossible for me to see the cause of his limp. In fact, now that I think about it, his whole outfit, from his flimsy hat to his musty jacket to his tattered pants, was brown, probably due to the forest dirt.

He pushed through the gate and made his way to the gardener, conveniently squashing some of the young herbs on the way. The gardener was watering the roses. On hearing the noise of twigs snapping, he turned, his eyes widening at the path of destruction this unknown guest was creating. 'Apples, mangoes, or bananas?' he asked. 'The mangoes are the sweetest in the country! And the apples! Oh, they can make anyone salivate. And the bananas...'

The woodcutter cut him off. Eyeing the gardener doubtfully, he said, 'You are the owner?'

'Of what, sir?'

'The garden, of course!'

'No sir, just the gardener.'

'Hmph. Thought so. You don't look like much.'

'Of course, sir.' Anyone could have heard the sarcasm in the gardener's voice. But the woodcutter didn't seem to notice.

'Is he around, then?'

'Who, sir?'

'Not so sharp, are you? The owner.'

'She is not around, no. May I pass on a message?'

'No, you may not. I have a secret for you. You can keep it, can't you?'

'But of course. Go on.'

'Sure? Well, then you know what a woodcutter is? That's me. And that mango tree there, its wood will bring more money than its fruit. So here's some money, now clear off. I will give you more when the job's done.'

I was shocked. Surely this man hadn't just said that he was going to cut me down! But he had. I had heard so with my own ears. My life was in the gardener's hands. Surely he would remain faithful to me! Anyway, if not, there were so many other flaws in this plan. The gardener *must* be clever enough to see that this woodcutter was too sly to keep his word! And, to my great relief, he was.

He smiled regretfully and said, 'Nobody will pay you anything for this tree's wood as it will remain attached to the fruit and the roots in this garden. Now here's your money and clear off yourself, or I will call the mistress. Goodbye.'

And that was the last I ever saw of the woodcutter.

After that, my luck really turned.

That day, the queen was riding past. It so happened that the tyre of her car was punctured. While waiting under my shade, she caught sight of my fruits, hanging past the garden walls. 'Oh!' she exclaimed, 'I must have that mango!'

So the minister came knocking on the door of the gardener, demanding a mango for the queen. The mango was presented, and the queen loved it so much that she had me uprooted and planted in her own garden! And put a picture of me on the national flag! Oh, if only my friends back at the classroom could see me now! I am the country's emblem, the pride of the royal gardens—the mighty mango tree!

my first friend

Vyomesh U. Tewari, Age: 13, Noida

Memories are strange things. They turn foggier and foggier as time passes, slowly begin to fade and then are lost altogether. However, whenever they resurface, they can bring enormous bliss and happiness. They can also bring you anguish and pain, reminding you of things so painful, so full of sorrow that they are better left in oblivion. Thus, it is natural that when a special memory resurfaces, that too from your childhood, you may get lost in it and just try to snake your path through all the mist to figure out what really happened.

It was just another day in the life of a small, obese boy living in Noida. I wasn't the most dashing of boys—neither the fittest, nor the brightest nor the most fun to hang out with. Other children avoided me like the plague, and whenever I tried to join their games or take part in their discussions, they would give me the most malicious of glances and entirely ignoring my existence—even if I stood just three feet away from them—they would run off to do something more engaging than wasting time with 'little hippo'. They boycotted those who tried to befriend me, and honestly, I never really knew why they hated me so much. I foolishly tried to keep being part of their group until something happened which changed my life forever, and became my most cherished childhood memory.

I never was much of a reader before that day. To me, books were just pages and pages full of words, which were of no use to me. I have to sheepishly admit that I had never even seen the inside of a book till then. Even my school textbooks I plodded through with great difficulty. But in the midsummer of 2007, when all the other children were busy with football in the local park, something changed in the life of a seven year old. I had, once again, in my foolish attempts to make friends, tried to join them in their game. My girth allowed me little flexibility and I knew it; their laughs and smirks rubbed it in deep all the same. I came back to my room and sat sulking in a corner, feeling miserable and lonesome. My mother's attempts to cheer me up were in vain. So she left the room, figuring I needed a little time alone.

By my side, in the bookrack on the bottommost shelf, was kept a wee little book. (It belonged to the time of one of my father's early efforts to initiate me into reading. Of course, all his attempts resulted in failure.) In my childish mind, I thought that I would show those bullies that I could survive without them. So I picked up that little book, and went through the first page. It was over before I knew it. Eagerly, I flipped the page, and the second and the third were read just as quickly. My body was feeling a new flow of energy. Every part of it was quivering with excitement. My brain was flushed with pure pleasure, and that was the moment I discovered the magic of books. That sudden excitement, the urge to explore deeper and deeper into something was the most delightful feeling ever. I was ecstatic. I was flipping through the pages as if my life depended upon it. Those beautifully woven words were bringing peace to an otherwise troubled heart. When my mother came back to the room, she gazed at me with wonder and smiled, which just added to that feeling of bliss. I was no longer lonely.

It was a strange thing. As I said before, memories have a tendency to turn foggy. I don't even remember the title of the book, the publisher or what the book was really about. The only thing I remember was that tears had welled up in my eyes. I had found a friend who would not tease me, mock me about my weight, give me malicious glances, shout at me or grow impatient with me. In short, it would not treat me as a worthless little boy, but as an equal, as a close friend.

That year, I went on to read the Amar Chitra Katha comics. In the year 2009, I began with classics such as *Robinson Crusoe* and *Treasure Island*, and before I knew it, I had started Charles Dickens. My reading skills grew and grew and grew, and my appetite for good books knew no bounds. I had at last found a friend who would never grow tired of me. Whenever this memory of my childhood resurfaces, I can see that little, friendless boy sitting on the sofa, going through his first ever book getting acquainted with something that was going to be his constant companion for the rest of his life.

the missing rat

Neha Kalia, Age: 13, Dehradun

It was a weekend in January. Now, here is something you should know about me—I love weekends. They are the most delightful days ever. For five whole days I wait for Saturday and Sunday to come by. On these days, you can sleep as late as you want (if your mother doesn't decide to shake you out of bed in the meanest ways, that is), there isn't any school to go to—you don't have to get out of bed and rush off to that miserable education centre, with only double maths to look forward to... Well, I could go on about the significance of these sacred days for hours, but let's move on with the story.

It was twelve in the afternoon on Sunday. I was fast asleep. (Heck, what do you expect, it was a Sunday!) Everybody in my family is big on sleep. In fact, a crane could hoist the roof off our house and we wouldn't even notice. I am a bigger fan of sleep than the others in my family and I can go to extreme lengths to make sure that I get my total quota of twelve hours of sleep. An example of this would be the time when Mom asked me to get up early to visit Grandpa. Have you ever heard of scented candles? They are much more useful than most people think. I just lit them in one isolated corner of my room and went back to sleep, accidentally setting off the fire alarm. While my family searched for the thing that had the potential to burn the house down, I slept ever-so-peacefully. I'm sure now you've got the gist of my sleep-obsessed nature.

Anyway, trying to wake me up before noon on Sunday is

like poking a bear in hibernation. But that morning, I woke up super early. You might wonder why. Here's the reason: I felt a presence in the bed next to me. A smelly, furry presence, and no, it wasn't my brother's disgusting foot. It was worse. The fact that I can detect a presence in my sleep would be considered useful by most people, but I found it exceedingly annoying.

I didn't realize what was happening at first. I snuggled peacefully in my sheets, feeling nice and lazy, when I felt the thing next to my face. I assumed it was my brother, tickling me with a feather. (Trust me, it wouldn't be the first time he was doing that.) I waved my arm around, trying to swat him away, but my hand only passed through empty air.

The furry thing moved across my face. Now I was really angry. I knew that if my brother was behind this, he wouldn't be leaving the room alive. I would behead him with a pair of safety scissors. I popped open one eye, then another, groaning as I stretched on my bed. Half of me, wait, let me rephrase, ninety-nine per cent of me, didn't want to move. The other traitorous one per cent was telling me to get up and investigate the matter. Guess which part won?

I flopped back on to the bed, closing my eyes. I could wait for a few hours to kill my brother; he wasn't going anywhere. I dozed off.

I rose from my bed at around two, when Dad decided to bribe me with doughnuts to make me get up. As I walked down the stairs to the dining room, I heard my elder brother yelling. I stopped by his room to see what the commotion was about. A word of caution, my brother is a science student and the biggest nerd ever. He loves Biology, Physics, Trigonometry and anything that involves brains. So yeah,

we're total opposites.

'What are you so upset about?' I asked groggily.

'My lab animal...I lost it. I'd brought him home to show Mom and...' he looked a little confused, before adding, 'I showed it to Mom in your room.'

That sentence sparked a memory. A memory that I wish I could delete from my life.

'That animal...did you get a tiger, or a frog?' I asked hopefully. 'Or maybe a kitten?'

Please God, don't let it be a mouse, I prayed silently.

'Why would I dissect a kitten?' he asked. 'It was a rat.'

And then, all hell broke loose. I screamed and rushed towards the shower, all traces of sleep gone. A rat—a filthy, furry rat—had been crawling through the blankets of my bed.

After that, the afternoon was a blur. I used each and every brand of disinfectant I could find on my clothes and bedsheets, called termite control and got my room vacuumed. I told my brother about his stupid rodent and guess where he found the rat? Inside my pillow!

So yes, that is how Detective Neha solved the case of the missing rat. And since that fateful day, I have made sure that my bed is thoroughly examined before I touch it.

Note to self: Make sure that dear brother never, ever enters my room without a complete security check, involving a metal detector, a search through all his belongings and a rodent scanner. Also, make sure to release a flesh-eating piranha in his bed.

the bond of hearts

Ankish Raj Prajapati, Age: 12, Lucknow

Sunil Dada, a little over seventy years of age, was the most neglected person in that house. He was like a forlorn orchestra to whose music no one dances any more. He had a son and a daughter-in-law. They had had a daughter, Sia, who was seven when she had died. That was two years ago. Sia was the only one in the house who had understood him, or had any time for him. She used to play with him every evening and listen to his stories. She used to love Sunil Dada's stories. She loved the way the protagonist would ultimately find a way out of the evil one's trap; the way the climax would always show the triumph of good over evil.

After her death, Dada was left all alone. He wanted to go live in Haridwar and devote the remaining days of his life to God. But his son did not want this. What would the world think if Dada left? He feared that people would say he got rid of his father by sending him away. So Dada spent his empty evenings sitting on a chair in the garden, reminiscing about Sia.

One such evening, he was sitting all alone. Winter was setting in. Usually, the main gate of the house remained open at this hour. On the road outside walked a little girl of seven. She lived next door. Her eyes met Dada's. To him, she seemed to look exactly like Sia—similar eyes, the same angel-like innocence. He raised his hand and motioned her to come to him. She was a little hesitant at first, but then

she came. Her little feet took the longest possible steps.

'What is your name?' Dada smiled and asked her.

'Megha,' she replied in her shrill voice. There was a slight tremble in it.

'Don't be afraid. I will not harm you. You can call me Dada.' He put his hand on her head.

'Megha, Megha! Where are you?' a voice came from next door.

'Mummy is calling. I have to go,' Megha told Dada.

'But promise me you will come to meet me here tomorrow,' Dada held out his hand.

'Promise,' she said, putting her tiny hand into Dada's. Then she was gone. But as promised, she came the next day.

'Why did you call me, Dada?' she said.

'Do you like stories?' Dada asked in his gentle voice.

'Yes, my grandfather used to tell me stories. I like those stories that have evil people troubling a good boy or girl. I love the way the children save themselves.' Truly, she was a replica of Sia, Dada thought, with a hand on her cheek.

'Where is your grandfather now?' he asked. She only pointed towards the sky where a few stars were beginning to peep out. There was a moment of silence. 'So, shall we begin our story?' Dada broke the silence and smiled at Megha who simply nodded.

He told her the lovely story of Hansel and Gretel. After it was over, Megha went home. And so the cycle continued. She came every evening, listened to a story, then went home. Sometimes, they would simply talk and share each other's thoughts and opinions. Megha asked Dada any question that came to her mind. Day by day, they grew closer to each other and they developed a very deep bond. Dada had found a new companion, a reason to continue living. Megha, too, had found herself a new grandfather. They both filled a void in each other's life. But fate was not in their favour.

One evening she told him, 'Dada, I am leaving this city.' The words fell like a bombshell on Dada. 'Where are you going? Why?' he questioned. 'Papa has got a transfer notice. We are going to Delhi,' she replied.

'When are you leaving?'

'Tonight at eleven thirty. We are going by train.'

Dada was heartbroken. He felt a searing pain in his chest, but showed no sign of agony on his face. He went in and reappeared with his fist folded. 'Give me your hand,' he told the girl. She held out her hand and he emptied the contents of his fist on her palm.

'These are my last savings, my blessings. Use them wisely,' he said with a sad smile. It was one thousand one hundred and fifty-one rupees. 'I will not use them. These will always stay with me,' Megha said and hugged him. 'I will miss you, Dada.'

'So will I, beti,' Dada said, as tears streamed down his cheeks. 'God bless you.' And in his mind he added, 'If there is any. If there was one, He wouldn't have given me another granddaughter only to take her away from me.' After she was gone, he shifted uncomfortably in his chair. He leaned backwards and closed his eyes in the hope that he would open them to find Megha in front of him, saying, 'I am not going, Dada. I will stay here with you forever.' But little did he know that he would never lift his eyelids again.

How was it possible? How could two people with no blood ties become so deeply bonded? Perhaps because bonds are not decided by blood but by the heart. So powerful, yet foolish and sensitive, is the heart of man.

champ goes to the zoo

Rishabh Bezbarua, Age: 8, Bangalore

'Bow-wow, bow-wow.' How I wish I could understand what Champ says. Who is Champ? Champ is my pet dog, of course! And my best friend. He is just like me. He likes what I like to eat, he wears clothes like mine and he even has glasses like mine.

I was always sad that I could not understand Champ's words and talk to him. One night, a fairy godmother asked me what I wanted. Immediately, I said that I wanted to talk to animals. Later in the morning, I was able to understand Champ.

The first thing Champ said was that he wants to go to a zoo. I asked my mother which zoo Champ and I could go to. She said the Hyderabad zoo is the best. So Champ and I booked two plane tickets to Hyderabad. We checked into a good hotel. Then, after breakfast, we went to the zoo. First we had a chocolate and an ice cream each. Then we went to see the peacock. I could understand everything the birds and animals were saying. The peacock said that it can fly. Immediately Champ replied that we, too, had flown to Hyderabad. They got into a fight. I told Champ we came by plane and did not really fly but Champ said that he loved showing off.

Then we went to the tiger's cage. The tiger warned Champ that if he came any closer, he would eat Champ. Champ replied, 'You can only eat me if you come out of that cage.'

BARK
BARK
BARK

This started a second fight. I quickly dragged Champ away to the lion's cage. But Champ called him 'Mane Man' and that made the lion angry. So another fight started. At the zebra's cage, Champ called the zebra 'stripy' which made the zebras angry. And so it went.

We went to look at the turtles. They were moving very slowly. This made Champ say that the turtles were going to die. The turtles said that they could live for a hundred years. Champ argued that it was impossible. This started another fight. Finally, when we reached the monkeys' cage, the monkeys started making faces at Champ. He got angry and started barking loudly. This only made the monkeys make more faces. So Champ also started making faces. But his glasses kept falling off whenever he made a face. That made the monkeys laugh. Champ gave up and said that he wanted to go back home.

Later, I asked Champ why he fought with everyone. He said he did not know why, but he enjoyed fighting. Then I asked why he didn't fight with me. Champ said I was his best friend and dogs never fight with their best friends.

Now I am very happy because while we eat and drink together, take a bath together and sleep together, we can also talk to each other.

the church of dahl and blyton

Meenakshi Kumar, Age: 16, New Delhi

As a child, I was highly ambitious and enthusiastic (in stark contrast to what I am as a teenager). During the summers, I spent every waking moment exploring the world, frolicking around with my best friend, Ojal, and my new neighbour, Ragini, whom we had decided to show the ropes to (us being veterans, having spent five of the eight years of our lives in the same colony). Every summer, we picked an activity and our lives would revolve completely around that.

One year, it had been the Terrific Twosome (inspired by the Famous Five), which was basically Ojal and me stalking 'suspicious' folk. The fun part was our definition of suspicious. It could be the Association of Annoying Aunties, the ones who pulled our cheeks hard and said, 'Aww cho cute' every time they saw us. It could be the older kids, who were too mature to allow us to play with them. But our dream suspect was ANYONE with a moustache. A bushy moustache, and you were an outright Gabbar Singh-esque villain for us. A simple one, and you were sneaky and slimy, out to kidnap all the innocent little children of the colony, stuff them in a truck and dump them in a shanty that for some reason, we always imagined had puke-green walls.

But this year, we had grown up. We were too mature to follow people around and too cynical to battle crime. Let Shaktiman come to the rescue. We had been caught too many times by aunties who did not value our vigilantism.

This year, we were studious, we were ambitious.

Now the one thing I loved more than plotting how I would rescue all of us if we were abducted, was reading. I devoured Enid Blyton, and if I ever saw the ground Roald Dahl tread on, I knew I would worship it.

I kept trying to get Ojal interested in the books I read but she was busy conducting surveys to find out if chocolate ice cream might actually be better than strawberry. I turned to my neighbour Ragini to get her to revere my beloved books. No luck there either.

One fine Sunday, tired of my incessant complaints about their behaviour resembling that of an unlettered baby, my dear friends came up with an idea. It created the best memory of my childhood. Born from my love of books and their love of me, was a thought that was entirely possible and grandly rational in the naïve mind of a child. We would (drumroll) start a library—collect all the books in existence, start the world's best library for children of all ages in the two shelves of the wooden cupboard I shared with my brother. Giddy with excitement, I hopped over to my house and narrated the idea to my mother (with a lot of clapping and giggling serving as background music). She hesitated a second before being delighted that I was taking on something that could not justify a restraining order. She pledged her full support.

And thus started the adventure of a lifetime. I collected all my books, sneaked into my brother's study room and 'borrowed' some of his, then went around the colony asking people to contribute to our noble venture. We used our cuteness knowingly and willingly. All you had to do to gain membership was contribute at least two books. By Monday afternoon, we had a respectable number of books and were ready to get

ADVENTURE
STORIES

started. All the books were piled up on my bed. My mother, Ragini, Ojal and I sat around in a circle, separating them into heaps according to age groups. We then assigned codes to the books, noted down the titles in registers and probably created an atmosphere more professional than our school libraries had ever seen. Arranged in perfect rows, by genres, then author, then height, our library was ready.

Meanwhile, we were also busy convincing people why this library was *the* place to be, enlisting last-minute subscriptions, advertising it on the colony's notice boards. Having made all arrangements and planning out everything remotely relevant to the functioning of the library (open on Wednesdays from 5:00 to 6:00 p.m. and at all hours on weekends, but it would be safe to call and confirm that I wasn't in Big Bazaar), we decided it was all systems go. We planned a grand inauguration party. Everyone turned up for the function and we cut a fancy white ribbon, feasted on popcorn and showed off the shelves we'd decorated and the registers we would maintain.

Surrounded by friends, my ever-supportive family and my books, I knew in that moment that if I could only work for it, I could achieve anything. The world was my oyster. And the warm glow that I felt in that instance told me, to quote a rather motivating song, that if I can dream it, then I can do it. If I just believe it, there's nothing to it.

My library lasted for more than a year and a half. The number of members grew with time. And eventually, I found my brethren at the Church of Dahl and Blyton.

a whole new world

Mallika Gupta, Age: 15, New Delh

Her eyes fluttered open, her peaceful slumber interrupted by the merry chirping of birds. She was blinded by the light pouring into her eyes. She sat up, slowly looking around. Where was she? All around her, lush stretches of greenery spread in all directions. Soft damp grass tickled her dainty toes, and a cool breeze made her flowing hair flutter. She sat rooted to the spot, trying to figure out how she had gotten there. But no solution came to her mind. Slowly, her shock disappeared as the piercing beauty of the surroundings invited her to explore. The spirit of adventure that flowed within her blood suddenly gained momentum.

The girl sprinted towards a nearby tree that radiated with life. The sturdy thick trunk, scarred and punctured, held many secrets of past years. Each fold of the rough skeleton bubbled with words, telling a story of its own. They told the story of the owls which had nestled within their bosom, and the woodpeckers which had pecked on their skin. They whispered the story of those leaves that had taken birth in their motherly arms and the flowers that died. The tree seemed to weep for her children as she bent with age and lowered her branches to rest on the ground. She had lived for a thousand years and was old and tired, but she knew she still had a long way to go.

The little girl stepped into the shadow of the tree, struck by the amount of life it hid. The leaves she stepped on crackled, their tanned, wrinkled skins struggling to stay together, the life slowly draining out of their veins. Yet they did not seem sad, because the soil welcomed them, ready to become one with them. She lowered herself to the ground and watched the little ants at work, each one walking with a purpose. They carried loads much greater than their weight, yet were dedicated and uncomplaining. She began following them beyond the tree, till they disappeared into the ground.

The lost little girl looked up and spotted an iridescent light not far off. Her lips parted into a smile as she rushed towards the calm lake. The shining nearly transparent water, too, hid a world within itself. Fish of different types and colours darted in all directions, playing with the naughty young tadpoles. The frogs seemed to be engaged in serious conversation, debating their opinions with loud croaks. On one edge of the lake, on a high stone, sat an aged turtle looking down at the proceedings, nodding occasionally as if to express his approval.

The sound of loud lapping caught the attention of the girl. Not far off, hidden under the shadows of the trees, was a white horse, more beautiful than anything the girl had ever seen. He was drinking the water from the lake, enjoying his drink so intensely that he did not see her approaching. As she reached out to touch his silky body, he neighed in surprise and trotted backwards. He turned to face her and his icy blue eyes pierced her skin. She stood silently, scared by the majestic creature as he inspected her. The monkeys in the trees above stopped their chatter and the birds stopped their songs. Even the leaves ceased their whistling and the winds forgot to blow. They all waited with bated breath, wondering what would happen. She looked at the horse with her big brown

eyes, her curls dancing on her face. She puckered her pink lips as if to apologize and soon the magic of her innocence touched him. He lowered himself on the ground in front of her, and she quickly scrambled on to his back. He rose and turned his head, looking at her as if for permission. She nodded and then he was off.

He quickly gained speed as she clung on to his mane for dear life. The forests and lakes rushed past and she squealed with laughter for she felt she was flying. Her excitement got the better of her and she let go of the magical creature. As her hands rose to her sides, she felt the horse slipping away. A moment of panic came over her and she braced herself for the pain of the fall. But it never came.

Her eyes once again jerked open, but this time there was no chirping of birds. Her eyes had not seen light for many years, and the cold beneath her feet was of a stone floor. Her curls, once so cheerful, were now dead and plastered to her thin face. She longed to be a bird so she could fly away. She longed to be a flame, brightly dancing alone, and envied the steam that made the air its home.

Her thoughts were soon interrupted by a whistle. In this world, she was not a young innocent girl, she was a fighter. She had been born in the factory, she worked in the factory. She knew no freedom.

A tear escaped her greying eyes at the lingering memory of her dream. She ached for a new life. She ached for a whole new world.

the sinking of the *norfolk*

Rishab Denis Rodrick, Age: 14, New Delhi

Between Denmark and Greenland lies one of the most fearful seas of all—the turbulent Denmark Strait. Countless ships have drowned in its waters. To those who managed to sail through it, it was like Dante's *Inferno*.

Here, on a cloudy mornin

g, during the Second World War, the following incident took place.

About ten miles off the coast of Greenland, one would find the raging waters of the Denmark Strait crashing against the silhouettes of a hundred sharp rocks. Sometime in the middle of the war, a British Royal Navy cruiser was spotted having difficulties in these rocks. The cruiser was the *Norfolk* and its captain was Sherman Court. He had been deprived of any sleep for three consecutive nights. The ship's engine had stopped working due to overheating and the *Norfolk* had simply been swept up by the angry sea for three days and dumped straight on to the rocks.

The captain knew that they were quite safe from German U-boats while they were grounded in the Strait, but if a German reconnaissance plane happened to discover a stranded ship—well, then that would be a different story.

Sherman was sitting idle when the bosun, Marshal Brown, came up to the bridge and slammed the door shut.

'It's damned cold out there, sir. It will be a long time before anyone shows up for help. The weather's worsening by the minute.'

The captain nodded and remained silent. The radio officer brought the captain a message. He read it and handed back the paper. His gaze shifted to the invisible horizon and remained there. The dark cloudy morning and the captain's silence made the bosun nervous.

'Where was the message from, sir?'

The captain remained silent but the radio officer, Patrick Jamieson, handed him the message. 'It's from the HQ, sir. Quite demoralizing.'

GERMAN BATTLESHIP AWARE OF YOUR CONDITION,
CANNOT HELP,
SHALL GIVE AIR SUPPORT TOM.
STAY ALIVE.

Marshal Brown crumpled the paper and threw it at his feet. 'What shall I do about it, sir? The engineer says we are shipwrecked, no hope for the engines.'

The captain spoke for the first time since morning. 'Double the men on watch, tell everyone to remain at action stations. The Germans wouldn't make us wait.' After a pause he asked, 'How many depth-charges do we have?'

Marshal wondered for some time then said, 'About twenty of 'em, sir.'

'When I tell you to, release two each on port and starboard. That should keep the U-boats at bay.'

The morning went by, so did the afternoon and then the evening. The crew was tired of standing in the cold and was now exhausted. Their eyesight too was becoming flawed.

The wind had risen but not enough to prevent an enemy attack.

The wait was over at six-twenty in the evening. A silhouette was sighted by a young lad of eighteen. He rushed to the captain to inform him of doom.

All the available guns were lined up to face the enemy, still fifteen miles away. The German battleship could not be recognized but it could be deciphered that it had come to a halt and had positioned itself well to align all its guns on the *Norfolk*.

The *Norfolk's* four fifteen-inch guns were all locked on the same range. Marshal, Sherman and Jamieson were the only ones on the bridge. Captain Sherman had the mouthpiece in his hand and he eyed the German vessel with extreme dislike, though his face remained calm. The German vessel was pitching in the waters whereas the *Norfolk* was steady between the rocks. His ship, Marshal knew, was an easy target—a sitting duck. Sherman couldn't wait any longer. He commanded his men to fire and then continue firing till death overcame either them or the Germans.

The first salvo missed completely. The Germans, with their accurate firing, paralysed the *Norfolk* with eight sixteen-inch shells. The battle was almost over. The engine room, the crew's quarters and the bridge—all were shot out of business. Almost all had died; some were thrown overboard only to drown minutes later, while the injured died of excessive loss of blood. But the eternal Sherman still remained, he rose from the remnants of the bridge. He was the lone man breathing. At first he appreciated the enemy's accuracy, then he assessed the damage to his own ship. The *Norfolk* was already leaning towards the portside. Its bow was almost overcome by the sea. The ship wouldn't sink completely, Marshal knew, for it was immovable in the rocks, but the blazing fire would surely choke the vessel. The Germans didn't bother to fire another salvo; it would have been a waste of ammunition. They left, and Marshal chose to die with his ship...

The next morning was calm. An RAF reconnaissance plane searched the area only to find a huge mass of burnt metal, still wedged between the rocks.

my best friend is an alien

Krishna S. Girish, Age: 12, Bangalore

My best friend Zozo is an alien. He has been living on Earth in the form of a human being for the last 233 Earth years, not revealing his identity to anyone. He feels we earthlings distrust all aliens. But recently, Zozo decided to go ahead and admit that he is indeed an alien, come what may. He then realized that all his secrecy was in vain. Even when he revealed the truth, nobody believed him. Nobody except me, of course. He is my best friend and he would never lie to me.

This summer, Zozo decided to take a trip home to Jupiter to meet his family. When I heard this I was heartbroken as I would have to spend the summer holidays without him. All my zillion plans were about to become zilch without him around. He noticed me moping and made me an offer that I just could not refuse. Did I want to go with him to Jupiter? Of course, it took me twenty-four hours to convince my parents that Zozo was indeed an alien. My mom was as thrilled as me to be the first human beings to travel beyond the moon and into outer space. My dad was not completely convinced, but neither did he want us to have all the fun without him. And we never go anywhere without Medha, my sister. So the travel party included the four of us, led by Zozo.

We drove to Halebid, a space launch station masked as an old heritage temple. We pulled on the space suits provided by Zozo. He then took a form I had never seen before. He became a gloopy greenish humanoid form. He saw my

TA-DA!!

amazement and decided to keep his old grin on for my sake. That was comforting. Before we realized what was happening, we were flying—past the moon, past Mars. Big Jupe, as Zozo called it, took a travel time of 23 minutes and 34 seconds.

As we were approaching, Zozo exclaimed, 'Oh, no. Not good.' I asked him what was wrong. He said there was a malfunction in the Gardicropal Crop of Enginnial Carderry, near the engine. We plummeted towards the ground as Jupiter's gravity pulled us in. 'Hang on!' Zozo yelled. 'We are landing in the Great Red Spot!'

The Great Red Spot, as everyone knows, is a never-ending storm of all kinds of gases and things like that, primarily hydrogen. Zozo handed me something. It was a glass jar. 'Capture the storm in it as a memento!' he said. I did as I was told. I now had a bit of swirling storm in a glass jar.

Zozo pulled the spacecraft out of the Great Red Spot and landed. When we emerged on Jupiter, it was very difficult for us to walk due to Jupiter's higher gravity. I weighed 75.6 kg there as opposed to my 32 kg on Earth. We visited four of the seventy-three moons of Jupiter. Zozo's great aunt lived on Ganymede, the moon that was bigger than Mercury! I remembered our own beautiful moon and the magical light that it sheds. Europa was comparable in size to our Moon.

Zozo brought us back to Earth after just twelve hours on Jupiter. That was 144 Earth hours, or twelve days!

Now, Zozo and me are back in school in the seventh grade. Zozo will always be my best friend on Earth. And on Jupiter too.

lost

Yuga Banerjee, Age: 9, Mumbai

My legs felt like jelly as we got off the aircraft. It was the first time my brother and I were travelling alone. We had arrived in Singapore and were visiting our cousins Tara and Nayana.

We sat in a bus. It was a long ride to their place. Both of us dozed off. We were awoken by the bus conductor hollering, 'Everybody off the bus! We have reached our final stop!'

'Final stop?' gasped Bhaiyya. We had lost track of place and time and had missed our stop. With no choice left, we stepped out into a bustling street corner.

Suddenly, my hand slipped out of my brother's grasp. In a split second, I found myself next to a burly unshaven taxi driver about six feet tall. He started rambling in what I thought was Mandarin.

'Sorry,' I said. 'I don't speak your language.' He shrugged and walked away.

I was reduced to tears and in a trembling voice I shouted, 'Shourya Bhaiyya, where are you?'

I gathered all my courage and thought hard. 'Phone! I need to make a call!' I looked around, hunting for a restaurant or a telephone booth. Aha! There it was. I quickly rushed inside and slammed the door behind me. I dug my hand inside my purple sling bag. Tears were flowing down my cheeks, blurring my sight.

'Where are the coins Papa gave me?' I spoke aloud irritated. 'Finally!' I barked. I snatched the phone off the

hook and punched in the numbers. I held the receiver up to my ear and this is what I heard: 'The number you have dialled is currently unavailable, please try again later.' Another tear trickled down my cheek and splattered on to the phone.

Now my courage gave way. My world seemed to have come to an end. What should my next move be? I spotted a police station. Was that Shourya Bhaiyya in there? I charged in, ignoring the buzzing traffic around me. I threw my arms around him. Looking up I saw a confused boy looking down at me.

'Oh sorry,' I muttered as my face turned crimson.

Stuck in an alien land and nowhere to go!

I didn't think of talking to the cops. I walked out and sat on the curb sipping a juice I had picked up at the corner store. I was nauseasous, tired and shaken. I was like a snail trying to hide in its shell.

It must have been a few seconds, minutes or hours till the silence was shattered by blaring sirens. I looked up and saw police cars screeching and stopping around me.

'Srishty! Srishty! Srishty!' That sound was music to my ears!

Was it a mirage? Was it Bhaiyya?

'Bhaiyya!' I broke down and hugged him.

After hearing my woes he told me to take a deep breath and stop wailing. At that moment, my uncle's car pulled up and the door swung open. He was an angel sent from heaven!

We jumped in and sped ahead leaving all the traffic behind. The car was warm and quiet. The minute we were on the clear road we were showered with hugs and kisses.

When we reached home we all tumbled out of the car and into the elevator. As both the boys dragged in the suitcases

I ignored them and ran into my favourite apartment, 0303 Waterside, shouting out to my aunt and cousins.

What an adventure that was!

son of humayun

Vishrut Kumar, Age: 13, Mumbai

Abhishek's mind was swirling. All the information about different Mughal kings that he had studied just the previous night rushed around in his head. Yet he was stuck on that one question, 'Who was Humayun's son?' Abhishek could not believe it. All the hard work that he had done last night had gone down the drain. Playing *Empire Ruler* on the Internet had provided him with valuable information about the Mughals—like how to defeat conquering hoards of foreign invaders, what weapons were used, and how buildings were built—but nowhere was it mentioned who Humayun's son was. (Taking the book out of the cupboard would have required a massive amount of will power which he could not muster.) And now in the examination paper there was the question and he was stumped. He decided to go with Jahangir; Akbar, as far as he remembered, was Humayun's father. He wrote down the answer. To hell with it, he thought. It's just one question after all.

He could not have been more wrong.

◆

Abhishek twisted and turned in bed. Images of battles flashed through his head. Try as he might, they would not go away. Just as Abhishek was drifting off into a deep sleep, a flash of light went off in his head and he saw a man wearing a...was it a frock?...with a fancy turban. The man reached out and

pulled something. Suddenly, Abhishek found himself floating out of his body.

'Abhishek Mehta?' said the weirdly dressed man. Abhishek was stunned. How could this man possibly know his name? And why was he wearing such clothes? Was it some new retro style?

'Are you Abhishek?' asked the man again in a louder voice.

'Yes,' replied Abhishek, still puzzled as to how this man knew him. 'And who might you be?'

'I am the person you wronged, you impudent boy! I am Jahangir, the great Mughal emperor,' cried the man. A wronged emperor? And by *him*? Clearly his mind was playing tricks on him. But the so-called emperor's next statement put his doubts to rest.

'Are you not the boy who wrote I am the son of Humayun?'

'Um, yeah', Abhishek replied. 'And get a life man; that was a mistake for God's sake,' he added in a murmur.

'What?!' screamed Jahangir, drawing out his sword from deep within the folds of his gown.

'No, I m-mean I am s-sorry if you were offended by it. It was a mistake and it won't happen again,' Abhishek stammered, shrinking away, scared out of his wits.

'It better not, otherwise you will have to face the wrath of Jahangir,' the Mughal emperor said, putting back his sword, a look of contempt in his eyes. 'Tell me boy, do you know the number of tombs that I have built?'

'Sorry, but that's not there in any history book.'

'Never mind that, not that I remember it myself.'

Abhishek half smiled but was immediately silenced by a stern look from Jahangir.

'Do you know that I have laid down beautiful gardens

like Shalimar and Nishat? I had also installed a chain of justice for my people. I had helped bring peace to the Mughal empire and improved the conditions of my people,' Jahangir said. Abhishek nodded.

'Can you tell me in what condition they are?'

'Well, I haven't been to many of these places, but I can say for sure that the chain of justice does not exist any more,' Hearing this, Jahangir cursed in Urdu.

'The modern world! It doesn't know the value of history. No law and order any more either I suspect. In heaven I have been hearing about the decaying world and the worsening condition of mankind.'

'Well, it's not all that bad. We are making constant progress in science and...'

'Science is what is destroying the world! In our time we had none of your so-called refrigerators and production factories and other polluting creations and we had a nice life. Now you all have destroyed the world.'

'So what exactly do you want me to do?'

'Realize the beauty of your heritage. Save it. Don't forego everything just for some more luxury. Look around you, nature is full of beauty if only you take the time to notice it. Now go and spread the word. Oh, and remember on Level 36, the cannon ball followed by the fire-water blast combo should see you through,' Then, with a wink, he was gone and Abhishek's spirit floated back into him.

The next morning he awoke with only two thoughts in his mind. One, that he had to pay more attention to the state of the world, and two, and more importantly (though Jahangir would probably have beheaded him for it), that he had to reach Level 37 in *Empire Ruler.*

runaways

Raghunandan Sriram, Age: 12, Bangalore

Sanjay woke up one morning, fresh and happy. It was the summer holidays and that evening, he was going to Shimla for a week with his family. He was wildly excited at the prospect of living in a resort and exploring the place. The day wore on and the time came for their departure. Along with his sister Deepa and his parents, Sanjay waited for the taxi to arrive. Right then, Sanjay's father got a phone call. He talked for a long time, nodding and shaking his head gravely from time to time. After the call, he asked Sanjay and Deepa to come to his room.

'I am very sorry to say this, but it's cancelled,' said Mr Choudhury.

'What is?' asked Deepa.

'The trip to Shimla,' he replied. 'Our guide there just informed me that strange things are happening there. Many disappearances have been reported. I thought it wise to stay away and go there the next time we get a chance.'

'But this is preposterous!' cried Sanjay. 'We hardly ever go anywhere during the vacations and when we *do* plan to go, you say it's dangerous!'

'We are not going to Shimla and that is the final decision. Go back to your room, both of you,' said Mr Choudhury angrily. Sanjay and Deepa went back, cursing and muttering darkly.

'I'm leaving this place,' said Deepa. 'I want to go and explore Shimla. Of course, I might not get to live in a resort and see all the tourist spots there, but at least I'll be able to go. Are you coming with me?'

'Are you mad?' asked Sanjay.

'Are you coming or not?' asked Deepa hotly.

'All right then. Let's go.'

The escapade was planned very well. That very night, they ran away to explore a world of wonder, a world of beauty!

'What do we do now?' asked Sanjay once they were safely out of the house.

'I don't know. We just have to explore and see,' said Deepa.

So they walked aimlessly for some time. All they had with them was ₹200. The first problem was how to reach Shimla from the small town where they lived in. It was about 160 km from their destination.

'I vote we go by train,' said Sanjay, after some thought.

'Do you know the procedure of getting a ticket?' asked Deepa doubtfully.

'We don't need any procedure. We just wait for the goods train to arrive. Then, we hop on to the last compartment,' said Sanjay airily.

'That's a sound plan,' said Deepa, beginning to enjoy herself. 'Let's go.'

Very few people will believe this, but an hour later, Sanjay and Deepa were sitting comfortably on a pile of goods, enjoying the scenery. They 'ooh'ed and 'aah'ed and saw some beautiful sights, which they felt they would never have got to see elsewhere.

'You know, this is fun,' said Deepa.

'That was a late realization, you know,' said Sanjay grinning.

◆

A few hours later, the train screeched to a halt. A board with the station name came into view. It read:

Station Multanpur

Shimla: 7 km

'This is where we get off,' said Deepa excitedly.

They sneaked out and, after asking a passerby the way to Shimla, started walking in that direction.

Very soon they were there. They spent the rest of the night sleeping in an abandoned hut.

The next morning, they started exploring the hill station. Never had they seen a place of so much beauty. They wandered around the hillside and ate a variety of new food at a small hotel. At the end of the day, when neither had a penny, or in this case, rupee left with them, they started discussing their plan of action.

'Wasn't today wonderful?' asked Sanjay. 'It was like being exposed to a whole new world, very different from our boring life at the village.'

'I wish we could explore more, Sanjay,' said Deepa, her eyes shining. 'But all the same, I think we should go back home.'

'I'm with you,' said Sanjay. 'We'll board the next train back home. Agreed?'

'Yes!'

◆

The journey back home was as smooth as the journey to Shimla. Standing outside their house, Deepa asked her younger brother, 'Are you prepared to answer the million questions Ma and Papa will ask when we show our faces to them? We'll tell them everything, shall we?'

'You bet!' said Sanjay.

the actress

Adithi Sundaresh, Age: 15, Bangalore

The grass is always greener on the other side. No one felt the truth of these words more than Amelia. More than once, Amelia had wished that she could slip away. She didn't want to be an actress. No matter what her friends told her, it just wasn't all it was hyped up to be. Sure, it meant she got to shake hands with famous people and move out of her modest apartment into a studio in the suburbs. Her new life as an actress had its perks, but most days, Amelia wished she could rewind to the past. She hated having her make-up team fall over themselves every morning even if all she wanted to do was go for a walk. She hated having to be immaculately dressed even to step out to go to the market. But what she hated most was the paparazzi. Amelia couldn't even use a public toilet without the paparazzi finding out. It would be plastered in the papers the next day, 'A-Lister Stoops to the Level of the Public', followed by an article about whether '...a superstar like Amelia thought public facilities were hygienic enough for her use.'

This seemingly never-ending nightmare had started two years ago, when she had been selected by a director scouting her locality for 'star material'. The director was drawn towards her natural beauty and charm and had said that she would suit the role perfectly. Nine months later, *A Whole New World* was released, starring Amelia Stewart in her debut role as Maylissa Hopkins, a young lawyer who gets entangled in a case involving a serious theft. The movie followed the story of Maylissa as she realizes that the suspect has been wrongly accused. By going out of her way to help him, she gets to know the world of a lonely young man who works hard to make ends meet. Of course, all's well that ends well, and the movie ends with Maylissa winning the court case and marrying the suspect who has now been proven innocent.

The movie was an enormous hit and topped the box-office charts. Amelia was the new cake in town and everyone wanted a piece of her. Soon, she had offers ranging from playing an adventurer who journeys to Jupiter to a singer who loses her memory. The producers of animated movies wanted her to voice their main characters and advertising companies wanted her on national television. Exasperated, she finally accepted the offer from the director of *A Whole New World* to star in his next movie.

Now, three months into the making of the movie, Amelia wished she could back out. She was in the Bahamas, and had just finished shooting a scene where she was rescued from drowning by her co-star. As she excused herself to go dry off, a fight broke out between her co-star and director. After she had dried off and finished her lunch, her director called. They were flying back to L.A. in an hour. Puzzled by the sudden turn of events she tried to call her co-star. She was told that he was already on board his jet and would be departing shortly. Amelia hung up and began to pack.

Half an hour later, she sat in her private jet wondering what had caused this sudden departure. Her co-star's jet entered the runway in front of hers. She obeyed the crackling over the intercom from the cockpit to fasten her seatbelt for take-off. No sooner had the jet in front of hers lifted off the runway than its engines failed and it plummeted into

the ocean below. Amelia was dazed as an emergency team rushed into her jet and escorted her off the aircraft.

Time went by in a haze for Amelia. They flew back to L.A. and the next few days were spent in press meetings and court sessions. Her co-star had died in the crash and the director along with the jet and his entire crew was missing. As word of the fight that had broken out between the now dead actor and the director spread, Amelia was plunged back into the world of her first movie. Her director was suspected of having planned the death of her co-star, making it look like an accident. That he was missing added fuel to the fire. Through it all, Amelia tried to lay low as much as possible. She was an actor, not a lawyer, as she reminded the paparazzi who questioned her the day of the hearing. The hearing went around in circles and was then postponed to a later date.

Search teams were deployed world-wide and rewards were offered for any clues leading to the location of the director. As days turned to weeks, and weeks into months, Amelia's role in the whole affair took a backseat. She was finally able to take that much-needed vacation. Soon enough though, she began to miss her old life. She had all the luxuries—the money she'd made from her first movie took care of that. But now, she realized how much she loved to act. Sure, it was a lot of stress and it meant paparazzi following her everywhere, but it let her get away from reality.

A year later, *Missing* released, starring Amelia Stewart. The accused director was never found though. Maybe, if life was like the movies, he would've been proven innocent and would've married Amelia. Reality comes crashing down on people though. Perhaps the director is living his own happily ever after somewhere else on Earth, in his own new world.

the end of time

Manika Ajmani, Age: 13, Mumbai

I stood at the edge of the deck, letting the sea breeze embrace me, as the salty water splashed against my face and hands and the sun's warmth caressed my face. I left the world around me and entered one of my own, where I was alone and only my thoughts surrounded me. I dreamt of home and how I would soon be there, and my spirits lifted.

Suddenly, the whole ship shuddered and I snapped out of my daydream as I heard shouts and cries erupting from somewhere behind me. I turned around. The captain was screaming orders at the rest of the panic-stricken crew. I saw young children crying as their mothers rushed them beneath the deck and I immediately knew something was wrong. I had only seen such scenarios on television, when something terrible was about to happen.

I stared dumbfounded at the increasing chaos around me. What could have happened?

'Move away from the edge, girl! You'll get killed!' someone shouted at me. I moved away, running and stumbling towards the voice as the breeze whipped against my face and the water was harsher as it sprayed against my skin.

'We are all going to die! Lord, save our souls!' cried a woman as she knelt on the deck, her face wet with either tears or sea water, I couldn't tell. But I knew what was happening. Our ship was about to sink.

'Move!' I yelled at the grieving lady, grabbing her arm

and pulling her with me.

However, she only shook her head. 'Don't you get it? We will all die! It's a sign!'

'We won't die! Get into a lifeboat and you will be saved!'

The lady didn't respond, or even if she did, I couldn't hear her over the deafening creaking noise that followed.

'We're going down!' yelled the captain.

A wave of water engulfed me and the last thing I heard were screams and shouts, which eventually faded into silence.

◆

Shipwrecked. The word floated into my mind as soon as I opened my eyes. The first thing I saw was the blue sky above me. I felt something wet beneath me, and as I turned, I saw what it was. Blood.

A shriek escaped my mouth and it took me a while to clamp my mouth shut with my hand. I got up guardedly, placing my hands on the ground beneath me, but I slipped and fell roughly on to something soft. More blood. When I looked around I saw the body of the lady I had tried to help. She wasn't breathing and her hair was matted and fraying. She looked as if she had been dead for years. Even her clothes had been torn, and her face was rotting.

I screamed again, and this time I pulled myself off the ground and ran heedlessly away from what I had just seen. I ran until my feet gave way beneath me and I fell to the ground, breathing heavily. It was only then that I became conscious of my surroundings.

I was in a city. Or what used to be a city. It was completely abandoned and the buildings around me were crumbling. Yet surprisingly, it looked as if people had only just been

MEL'S
STORE
SUPERMARKET

living here. A few lights flickered from the windows of deserted shops and paper and rubbish were strewn across the streets. Whatever the reason was for the people here to leave this place, they had evidently left in a hurry.

But how did I end up here if my ship had sunk? Was I the only survivor?

My thoughts were interrupted when I heard the unmistakable rumblings of my stomach. I looked around. A store was positioned just across the road, its neon sign still flashed the words: 'Mel's Convenience Store. Open 24 Hours'. The name sounded awfully familiar.

An hour or so later, I had managed to find plenty of food. I had helped myself to boxes of cereal, beans, biscuits and canned fruits. Even the food tasted fresh. It was all too surreal and inexplicable.

I wandered further into this uninhabited city. How did this happen? Where was I?

'Hello?' I called out, but all I heard in reply was my own echo. There weren't even any birds or trees. It seemed like everything living had been wiped clean from the city.

After hours of exploring, the sun finally set and the stars came out. I sat on a wooden bench underneath a dim street lamp. On the bench lay a newspaper. I read the name: *The Times of Rosewood*. Another familiar name. I tried to think of where I had heard the name before, but everything before the shipwreck was just a blur in my memory.

I continued reading the paper, it was dated 10 October, 2013. The same day of the shipwreck, except ten years later…

I read the next headline: 'Tenth Anniversary of the *Cadenza* Shipwreck. Tribute to the Dead.'

Cadenza was the name of my ship.

I forced myself to read further, even though I felt sick to my stomach, and the world seemed to be spinning around me.

'List of the deceased: No. 13, Karen George.'

Karen George was my name.

That was all I saw before I collapsed into darkness.

my magic lamp

Anjali Chandawarkar, Age: 14, Mumbai

Magic. The only dream of mine that, at ten years of age, I wanted to turn into a reality. Anything to do with magic would make me sit up and listen attentively. I wanted to witness it, feel it just once! And my Dadi showed me that it existed in a lamp, the one that is lit as a symbol of hope and enlightenment, in the temple of God. You don't believe me? Well then, permit me to show you…

'DADI!' called out my ten-year-old self. 'Dadi, where are you? It's eight-thirty already! God will get angry if we don't light the lamp!'

Dadi (my paternal grandmother) smiled as she slowly walked towards me.

'Sorry, darling,' she said, as I smilingly handed her a matchbox and a can of oil. 'Dadi is getting a little slow now.'

'Don't worry, Dadi. I will help you,' I said, giving her a hug.

Dadi laughed and said, 'God bless you, dear.'

I fell silent as I watched my grandmother delicately pour the oil into the lamp, and then light the matchstick. My eyes widened in awe as I gazed at the tiny yet powerful ball of illumination that was bright enough to lighten up a whole room.

'Join your hands, close your eyes, Anjali, and let's feel some magic,' Dadi instructed. I quickly obeyed, my ears yearning to hear the soft voice in which Dadi sang her daily prayers.

I could feel the warmth of the lamp on my cold little hands; I could feel the pure devotion of Dadi's prayers, and the brightness that the little lamp was spreading. It sent a pleasant tingle down my spine.

That night, while I rested my head in Dadi's lap, listening to her soothing lullabies, I asked her a question that intrigued me.

'Dadi? Why does that little lamp feel so powerful every time we light it?'

Dadi stroked my forehead lovingly as she told me something that awed me no end.

'That lamp has magical powers, Anjali.'

I sat up like a spring. 'REALLY?!'

Dadi smiled and nodded. 'Really. But it only works for those who help others, behave like good girls, are always truthful and remember to thank God every day with their Dadis.'

I sighed. That sounded like a lot of good work for a fairly naughty child like me. But if that lamp had magical powers, then my ember of hope was not going to die out any time soon.

'I want to see the magic, Dadi. Will you help me?' I asked, looking for assurance in my grandmother's wrinkly face. Dadi smiled and nodded. 'As long as you follow what I say,' she added. I felt happy.

Every day for the rest of the year, I followed Dadi's instructions precisely, careful not to falter anywhere. Every day, I would hope eagerly that in the evening when we prayed, the lamp would show me its magic.

Finally, my eleventh birthday came and I was angry with Dadi and the lamp. Dadi had said it would work, so why

hadn't it? I had been so good all year, done my duties well, and had been appreciated so many times by Dadi herself.

While my parents couldn't make out why I was sulking on my birthday, Dadi came and sat down next to me.

'What can I do to make my little girl happy again on her special day?' she asked, pulling my cheek lovingly. I frowned at her and said, 'Dadi, you said there was magic in that lamp. Where is it?'

Dadi smiled. 'Anjali, magic doesn't show itself as fairies or spells or castles or princesses in real life. All that happens in stories.'

I still felt furious. 'So what happens in real life?' I asked sarcastically.

Dadi smiled. 'Look back on the last year. Whenever you did something good, didn't you feel that lamp shine brighter? Whenever you felt unhappy and confused, didn't that lamp restore your confidence by its warmth? That's magic in real life, darling. That lamp we light for God is so powerfully magical, it can make you feel appreciated when you do good work and comfort you during trying times.'

'So you're saying that's magic too?' I asked, softening a little.

Dadi nodded.

I thought back. I realized that the lamp had made me feel proud of myself every time I had done something good. It had burned brighter when I needed a reason to keep going, as if extending its arms to let me know that it was there for me. The lamp had become my friend, and had made my life happier, purer through its light… If that wasn't magic, what was?

That day is still clear in my memory. I believe that magic

exists, even in lamps. You just have to be good, pray sincerely and never stop believing. My lamp is a symbol of belief that magic exists in our lives in the form of purity, hope and devotion. My magic lamp makes me believe that anyone can achieve goodness, if they have something to believe in…

Do *you* have a magic lamp?

my classmate unnati

Ananya Kirpane, Age: 14, Mumbai

This incident took place on 20 July 2012. It's long ago, but I remember it as if it were yesterday. Back then, I was in the ninth standard. Fridays were special days, not only because it was the last day of the week but also because we had our PT (physical training or games) class on that particular day. Since we had recently moved into the upper secondary (ninth and tenth standards), the count of our PT periods had dropped by fifty per cent of what it had been in eighth standard, that is, we now had only one PT period per week. We were not particularly overjoyed by this development, but we made do. Another, far more interesting, happening was that six new girls had joined our school. Three were in the ninth standard. Out of them, two came to our class and one went to the other. This PT period was their first. So, as we made a line and filed towards the hall in silence, I decided to talk to the two new girls.

We reached the hall and were ordered to stay in line, while the monitors were asked to check whether the students had clean and neatly clipped nails. Our class had a set-up where every month, the monitors would change. That month I was the monitor. First, I got my own nails checked by the teacher and after getting the green signal from her, I proceeded up the line of girls inspecting the nails of my classmates. The monitors usually did not check very strictly as we wanted all our friends to play. As my eyes drifted past a series of clipped nails, they landed on one pair of hands that stood out from the rest. I looked up to find the owner of the eye-catching nails. It was Unnati, one of the two new girls. I whispered my compliments about her nails. She smiled at me like a proud mother does when someone compliments her child. I then moved on till the end of the line without bothering to tell the teacher about her unclipped nails.

A mere five days later there was a report in the news. It read:

Petrified of faring badly in a maths test at school, a thirteen-year-old girl committed suicide by hanging herself from the ceiling fan with her mother's saree the evening before the exam.

Unnati Jeswani, a ninth standard student of BARC school, which is located in the Anushakti Nagar campus in Trombay, left behind a suicide note on Friday, stating that she was frustrated and upset that she could not grasp the subject despite all the effort her parents and she had put in.

The note reads: 'Main padh padh kar pagal ho gayi hoon. Daddy ne bhi sikhane ki bahut koshish ki, lekin main ganit samajh nahin pati. Ganit ke alawa zindagi mein kuch nahin. Main apne maa aur pitaji ko aur sharminda nahin kar sakti. Main ghutkar nahin jee sakti. Mujhe bhagwan ke paas jana hain… Bye, Mummy. Bye, Daddy. [I am losing my mind trying to grasp maths. Daddy has also tried to teach me, but I can't seem to understand it. What will I do with my life if I don't understand maths? I don't want to embarrass my parents any more. I can't continue living like this. I am going to God.]

I refused to believe it when my classmates told me about the incident, not even when it was announced by the principal in the assembly. It was only after the news article was published that it slowly started to sink in. The first thought that came to my mind was, 'But that can't happen...she had such beautiful nails.'

This was a year ago. Even today, whenever I cut my nails or polish them or try in vain to shape them, Unnati always comes to my mind. She was not my best friend or even one of my close friends. She was just a girl who had smiled back at me when I had admired her nails. I hardly knew her for a month. I may not remember her face very well but I shall always remember her as the girl whose delicate hands had very beautifully shaped, neatly-cut and splendidly polished nails.

the day the world turned upside down

Aashna Rai, Age: 9, Pune

I always used to think it would be so wonderful if the world turned upside down and children could rule over parents. While our parents went to school, we would relax in front of the TV with a bowl of chocolates or crisps.

My mother always told me that, 'Whenever your heart desires a wish, wait for a full moon night. And as soon as you see the moon, wish for something and it will come true.' So I waited for a full moon night. Then I wished. 'Please God, let only one day of my life be turned upside down. That day will be the best day of my life.' Then I went to sleep.

The next day, when I got up it was eight o'clock. I was shocked that I had missed my school bus! Where was Mummy? She was supposed to wake me up. I had my science test that day. When I went to the master bedroom, I saw that both Mummy and Daddy were still sleeping.

I woke her up and shouted, 'Mummy, I missed school! It's past eight.' Imagine my surprise when she sleepily told me, 'Mum, please don't wake me up.' When I tried to wake up Daddy, I got the same reply. Then I understood what had happened. My wish had come true!

So I told myself, 'It's okay. Let's go and make ourselves some yummy breakfast.'

Breakfast was a disaster. I woke my brother up for help.

We didn't know how to toast the bread or use the microwave. So we all had cold bread with hard butter (just taken out from the refrigerator). Mummy grumbled and said, 'Mum, this breakfast is horrible.' I had to agree with her. Then it was time for us to take a bath. Just like us, our parents didn't move from their places. We had to literally push them into the bathroom.

The next thing to do was to clean the house. But as Mummy and Daddy wanted to play, I had to clean the house while my brother, Ritvik, took charge of going to the market to buy food for lunch. When he was back, I was done with sweeping the house clean.

Lunch turned out to be worse than breakfast. The rice was not properly boiled. We hadn't peeled the potatoes properly. And to make it worse, my brother had bought the wrong mangoes. They were sour. He then had to go drop Mummy and Daddy off to their tennis class. When they came home, I was too tired to make dinner. But still, I *had* to make it. While making bread for dinner again, I fainted…

I woke up with a start. I saw that I was in my bed. My mother was ironing my school clothes. She said, 'It's early! Seems like you had a bad dream.'

I was awestruck. 'Are you my mother again?' I asked her.

'Of course! I was always your mother.'

And then I realized that it had all been a horrible dream. And I understood how hard our parents worked to take care of us. Never ever did I wish for the world to be turned upside down again. I got up and went to help my mother.

the case of the missing phone

Trupti Anil Soman, Age: 15, Pune

My mobile phone is my most unfaithful partner. Whenever I want to call someone, it messages someone instead. Whenever I want to message someone, it shuts down automatically.

I've seen teens hooked on to their mobile phones. They text every millisecond and stay on the line for hours. I wonder how they do that. It seems nearly impossible for me.

My mobile phone never agrees with me. Suppose I want to call up a certain Mrs Roy, it decides that I should call up Mr Jones instead. Whenever I want to go out, it refuses to charge. Whenever I am in a hurry and want to call someone quickly, it freezes.

Let's just say we have a love-hate relationship.

One day, I was about to go out for my best friend's engagement party. I was all dressed up and covered in about two inches of make-up. I forced my large feet into the stilettos I had bought and took out my purse from the wardrobe.

As I was about to step out, my brother came running down the stairs and stopped me. Now, as per ancient Indian superstitions, one must never stop a person who is about to go out or the work that the person is going to do will be unsuccessful. I am normally not a superstitious person but I think that day, my luck went against me. So I turned around with an exaggerated sigh and asked my brother what on earth had happened for him to stop me.

'Mom said that you must keep your phone nearby as...'

he said, panting while clutching his sides.

'As what?' I asked.

'As...' He was still huffing and puffing.

'Neel, I am getting late. Hurry up and stop wheezing like an old lady.'

'As...'

'Oh, just forget it. I am going. Goodbye.'

'Wait! Can't I even catch my breath?'

'Yes, you can, but afterwards. Now tell me what it is. I can't be late for Sheetal's engagement.'

'Well, Mom said that she is at the hospital with Minu Aunty.'

'Who's Minu Aunty?'

'Minu Aunty is mom's friend's brother-in-law's wife's third cousin's friend's sister.'

'Oh, okay. So what's wrong with her?'

'Well she is seriously ill and might...'

Neel drew a line across his throat with his finger.

'All right. So what can I do?'

'You might have to go and pick up Mom and drop her off at Minu Aunty's for the last rites.'

'In these clothes? Everyone will stare at me.'

'It doesn't matter. So where's your phone?'

'Right in here.' I patted my purse.

'Are you sure?'

'Don't you trust me?' I pouted.

'I don't trust your phone. Give me your bag.'

I handed it over to him and he opened the zip and turned it upside down on the table. Promptly my make-up items fell out, but there was no sign of the phone.

'Aha! I knew it. Your phone is not here. Where is it?'

'But I just put it there.'

'No, you didn't. Where is your phone?'

'I don't know and I don't care. I am getting late for the party. Can you please pick up Mom if needed?' I made sad puppy eyes at him.

'No, I am not going to. Your phone has caused me enough trouble already. And anyway, I am going for a movie in half an hour.'

'You are my darling brother, right? You know how much I adore you.'

'Don't try your tricks on me. Let's look for your phone and then you can be off.'

'Okay.' I gave an exasperated sigh.

'Where did you last see it?'

'I don't remember.'

'Great. Maybe you should pop some memory pills first. Let's search in your bedroom.'

I nodded and we both went upstairs.

My bedroom was a mess, as always. My brother shook his head in disgust. I made a face at him.

I started by pulling my clothes off the bed, where they lay in a huge tangled mess. I managed to find three lost hair clips, five pencils and four rubber bands but no mobile phone.

My brother was meanwhile searching my study desk. He was shoving aside large piles of paper and heaps of pens, pencils and erasers.

'I would rather search in a garbage dump. It would be cleaner than your room.'

'Not my problem.'

'Yes it is. You *sleep* here. You should clean it from time to time. What is this? Oh my God! Your first grade report

card. What the hell is it doing here? What's this? Yuck, it's full of spiders.'

He dropped the box full of dead spiders on the floor.

'It's my fifth grade science project,' I said defensively.

'That was ages ago. And look at this. What the hell is… Yikes!'

He fell down, hitting my box of spiders as he fell. All the dead spiders rolled out on the floor.

'It's just a doll's head,' I replied, placing my hands on my hips.

'I am not staying here a moment longer. Your phone is obviously not here. This place is a dump.'

He got up and stomped out of the room. I followed him down the stairs.

'Maybe it's in the living room,' I offered.

'You have to search for it on your own. I am going out for the movie.'

'Please! I can't manage this on my own.'

'I am out of here. Goodbye.'

I watched dismally as he hurried out of the house. I gathered my dress around me and sat down on the stairs, flustered.

'What happened, beta?' Ram Manohar, our ancient gardener, who had just come in through the door, asked me.

'Nothing Ramji, I can't find my phone and I am getting late for my friend's engagement.'

'Such a small thing and you are getting worried over it so much? Today's generation can't even take a little bit of tension. What will happen when you go to your sasural?'

'Can you help me to find it?' I cut in before he could give me a long lecture on how to behave at one's in-laws.

'Sure, sure, let's search.'

We started searching in the living room. I tossed around the cushions on the sofa, the armchairs, the rocking chair, the table, even the ones on the shoe rack. My God, I never knew that we had so many cushions.

My mobile phone had clearly decided to play a complicated game of hide and seek.

Ramji searched around as well, coughing and wheezing. He coughed so violently when he was searching near the bookshelf that for a moment I thought that he would not live till the end of the search. When he was poking around our showcase, our family photo fell on him. Thankfully, he managed to survive.

I rubbed my tired eyes. I had been searching for over an hour. Sheetal must be red with anger by now. Anyway, I thought, it would be good for her. She was always so white and pale.

Just then the doorbell rang. Poor Ramji was sitting on the sofa and managed to slowly get up but I wasn't sure that he would last the trip to the door. So I rushed to open it myself.

Mom had come back!

'Is Minu Aunty all right?' I asked worriedly.

'Oh, she is fine. All she had was a bit of cold. So how was Sheetal's engagement? What did she wear? How is the groom? Who was wearing what? Who looked the worst? Who drank the most? Who ate the most? Who danced the sloppiest? Come on, tell me everything. I have brought some samosas for you.'

My mother dragged me inside.

'Hello, Ramji. Sit, sit. You don't look well. Do you want to go to the hospital? Or should I get you some good brandy?

I don't want you dying here on my new sofa.'

'Brandy would be good,' Ramji's voice came out in a whisper.

'Mom, are you sure you had gone to the hospital? Neel stopped me and said that I need to take my phone along but I had lost it again. So I spent an hour searching for it. I even missed the party. Sheetal will be so mad at me. And here you are, all happy and pouring out brandy. For God's sake, are you listening?'

My mom looked up at me, confused for a second, but when I lifted my eyebrows she answered.

'Oh yes, I am listening. I was at the hospital, you know. I was there for half an hour. Minu just had a cold. She just needed a little out of the bottle.' My mother winked at me surreptitiously. 'So I quietly poured her some. She got better in a little while and we went out shopping...'

'You went out *shopping*?' I interrupted her midway, flabbergasted.

'Yes, and we bought some very pretty salwar kameez sets. I bought one for you. It's light green.'

'Oh, forget that! Do you know where my phone is?'

'Yes. I have it with me.'

'But you told Neel that...'

'Oh yes, but then I realized that I had it with me all along. But I forgot to tell you. By the way, why didn't go to Sheetal's party? Why are you looking so pale? Are you all right? Oh my God, Ramji, she has fainted!'

So the case of the missing mobile phone was solved.

mission to kronos

Rohit Sahasrabuddhe, Age: 13, Pune

ESS *Achilles*, the pinnacle of mankind's technological skills, soared through the vast depth of the universe. She was bound for the planet Kronos. The name itself was a little intimidating, but it fit the planet perfectly. Telescopes aimed at it from Earth showed large, towering, black mountains shadowing vast, desolate plains. The preliminary scans had picked up large reserves of iron. Earth's iron resources had been used up by 2050, more than fifty years ago. Iron reserves on Mars were also depleting. Man desperately needed more iron.

ESS *Achilles* had a crew of four. Jock Carson, the American, was the mining expert. Rahul Mishra, the Indian, was the aeronautical engineer. Mr Tashikawa from Japan was the geoscientist. Wing Commander Hel was a Soviet pilot, the captain of ESS *Achilles*.

The silhouette of Kronos grew larger in the distance. Though he knew that the ship was a superior craft and he was confident in the capabilities of Eddie, the Artificial Intelligence computer running the ship, Hel was still a little worried. His sixth sense was tingling.

A week later, the giant ESS *Achilles* was in orbit. As the most important moment of their lives approached, the astronauts were in a state of nervous disarray. Everyone was anxious. They were huddled around a computer terminal on the bridge. Hel was desperately trying to reach Eddie. Manual landing of the ship was impossible. It had to be an

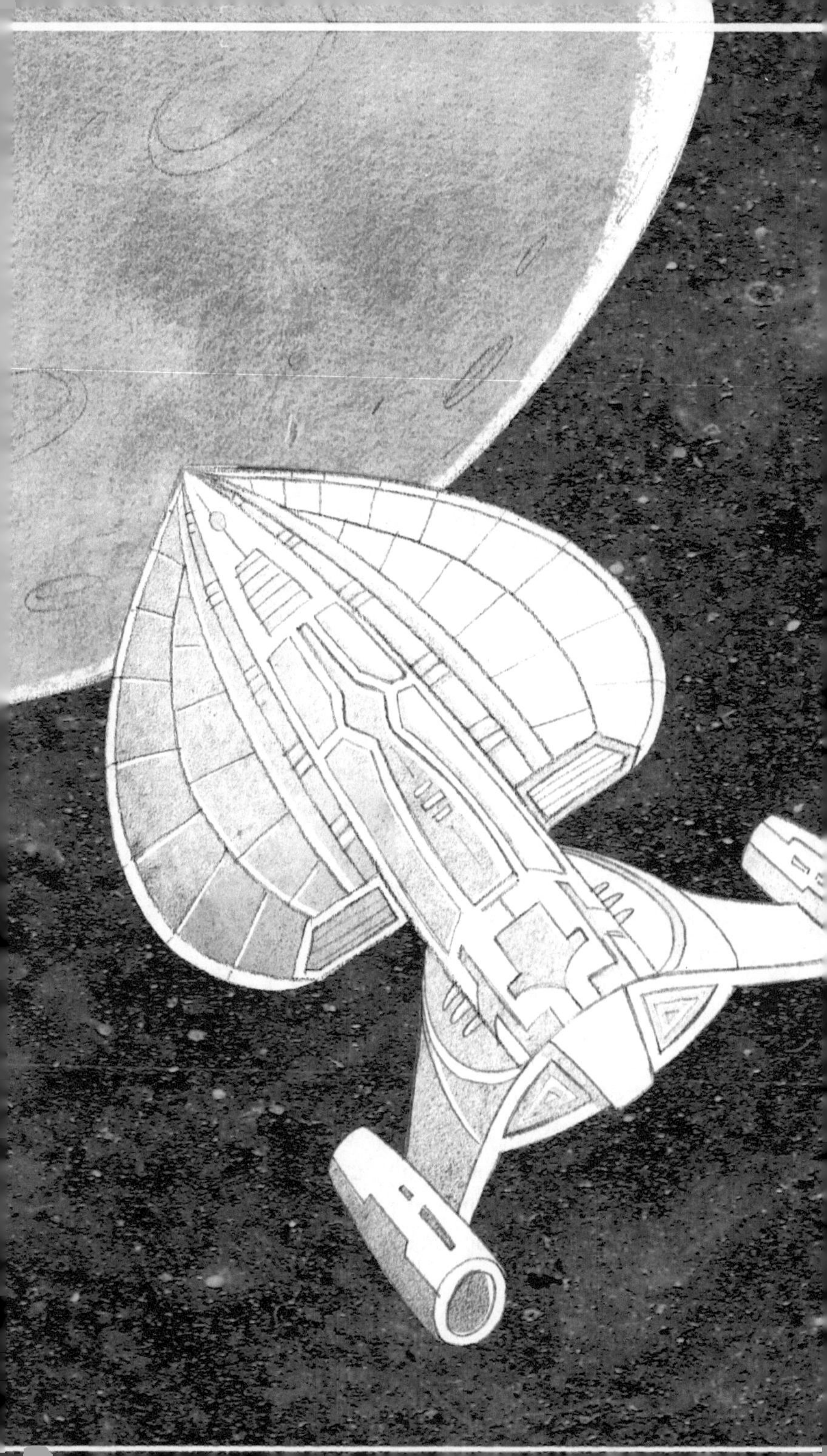

automated process. And at this critical moment, there was a fault in Eddie's motherboard.

As Hel feverishly tried to restart the computer, Tashikawa was pacing behind him.

'We need to get down there...' he was saying.

'Look, for the LAST time, I AM DOING EVERYTHING I CAN!' screamed Hel as he whirled backwards and glared at Tashikawa.

At this precise moment, the ship went dark. There was silence.

Back on Earth, Venkateshwar Iyer rubbed his hands in glee as he smiled at his computer screen. He flexed his fingers and typed in:

```
restart all systems code:101
```

The lights on ESS *Achilles* turned back on suddenly. The computer screen in front of Hel lit up and a soft voice said, 'Hello, Wing Commander. How are you?' Eddie was up and working again.

'Yes!' Hel breathed a sigh of relief as he looked at the clock. In another five hours, they would be on Kronos. 'Activate landing sub-process,' he said to Eddie.

'Activate landing sub-process,' said Iyer's computer in Hel's voice. Iyer smiled as he okayed the command.

'Landing sub-process initiated, descent in T minus 10 minutes,' said Eddie.

Five hours later, ESS *Achilles* touched down on Kronos. The ramp slid down smoothly and the bay doors opened with a loud hiss. A couple of rovers trundled out was on to the sandy surface of the planet. Man had reached Kronos.

The crew on Kronos left their ship. The rovers disappeared and the dust kicked up by their wheels settled down. All this was seen by a small camera and transmitted to Eddie.

On the bridge, Eddie's main console came alive. 'Initiating take-off sub-process…' said the computer. The bay doors hissed shut and the ramp was retracted. With a final roar, the engines reached maximum power and the ship sailed away, leaving its crew behind.

Fifteen kilometres away, the sound of the ship's engine had reached its crew. They turned around in surprise. In the distance, the harsh sunlight glinted off the retreating shape of ESS *Achilles*.

The astronauts were in a state of panic. Hel was the only one who had the situation under control. He walked towards the others. 'Well,' he said, 'we are stranded. I guess our best course of action is to find a way to contact Earth.'

Mishra stood up uncertainly. His eyes had the glint of a madman. 'Can't you see we've been left alone? CAN'T YOU SEE THAT?' He sank down with a moan and scrabbled wildly at his faceplate. Suddenly, the faceplate hissed open. With a gasp, Mishra sank down.

The crew of ESS *Achilles* had been reduced to three.

When they inventoried their supplies, the astronauts found that they had food for four months in the rover. So they had four months to find food and water. Their prospects were bleak.

They pitched camp. At night, Hel was awakened by a sound outside his tent. He peeked out. Carson was standing there, a dark silhouette, blocking Hel's view of the star-studded sky. In his hand, Carson held a pack of cigarettes. 'I need a smoke…' he muttered. Before Hel could leap out and stop him, Carson had opened his helmet. Hel looked away.

Over the next months, Hel and Tashikawa explored the planet Kronos. They created a rough map of the lay of the land. Food was running low. It wouldn't last for more than a week now.

They were exploring a cave when it happened. They were using some rope from the rovers to rappel down the shafts. The ropes were thin and worn from use. Hel was at the mouth of the hollow tunnel. Suddenly, the ropes holding up Tashikawa snapped. Hel looked down the mouth of the shaft in disbelief. Tashikawa was gone.

Hel was the only man alive on Kronos. He dragged himself to the mouth of the cave and out into the harsh sunlight of the sun. Too weary and shocked to think coherently, Hel slumped down. He knew that he wouldn't last long. Either starvation or insanity would get him.

From the muddled recesses of his mind, he suddenly remembered ESS *Andromeda*, the second spacecraft coming to Kronos. She would be there in a month! Maybe at last, he could be saved.

On Earth, Venkateshwar Iyer flexed his fingers and typed in:

```
access to ESS Andromeda
```

goddess of the jungle

Malavika Thampi, Age: 9, Thiruvananthapuram

I was resting my head on the pillow in my bedroom when suddenly, something sparkled near the window. It was a shooting star! At first, I was a little scared of it. Then it spoke to me:

'Dear Malavika, I am the star and goddess of the jungle.'

'The star and goddess of the jungle! Is it true?' I asked.

Suddenly the star turned into a fairy.

'Yes, I am the goddess of the jungle. I came here to tell you something important. The jungle is in danger. The evil monster Dinoking has arrived.'

'But what can I do? I have no magical powers. Maybe if I could talk to animals…' I said.

'I know. But you are the only one who can rescue us. So from now on, you will have the ability to talk to animals.'

I was happy.

The fairy asked, 'Can you get on my back? I will carry you to the jungle.'

'Of course. I will come with you.'

As soon as I spoke, I realized that I sounded like a bird.

'What happened to me?' I asked the fairy.

'Don't worry. I did this because you wanted to talk to animals.'

'I will rescue all of you. Let's go to the jungle,' I said bravely.

The goddess of the jungle transformed herself into the shooting star once again. The journey on the back of the

shooting star was really exciting. We went through the clouds and suddenly reached the jungle. There was a bad smell in the air. The shooting star became a fairy again and told me that the bad smell was from Dinoking, who had two red eyes, a black and scary horn and four log-like legs.

'Hmm...I have got an idea,' I said to myself. I called all the animals in the jungle. They were all very happy to see me. I told them how to trap Dinoking. At first, as per my instructions, the kangaroos and the pelicans collected many pebbles. The pelicans carried them in their beak bags while the kangaroos carried them in their marsupial pouch. Then we rubbed all the pebbles together and made fire. We dug up the soil and found sharp and stony materials with the help of the moles. Then we put all of them in a big vessel, boiled them, added salt and pepper and prepared a dish out of them.

That evening, we met Dinoking and served our dish. He said that it was delicious and that he liked it very much. He quickly finished off the dish. But he couldn't digest it and after some time, Dinoking ran hither and thither, crying in pain due to abdominal cramps. At last, Dinoking fell to the ground with a loud cry and finally died. We were all very happy and sang and danced together to celebrate the death of the evil monster. Everybody thanked me. I bid goodbye to all my jungle friends.

Then I requested the goddess of the jungle to carry me back to my bedroom. 'But first,' she reminded me, 'if you want to talk to humans you should change the sound of your voice!'

I burst out laughing.

diwali gift

Neha Rajan, Age: 14, Bangalore

Diwali, the festival of lights, the victory of purity over evil, had finally arrived in the buzzing city of Bangalore. There were lights everywhere, people were on a shopping spree, houses were being painted with fresh, bright colours—it seemed as if the whole city was rejoicing. But in a quiet, lonely corner of a small colony, there was a cloud of gloom. An orphan of about seven was crying inconsolably. She looked weak; she had probably not eaten for weeks. Her earliest memory was of waking up to a loud, screeching sound. She was trembling as she ran, ran as fast as her tiny feet could, away from that noise. Little did she know that the noise was from a blast due to a gas leak in one of the houses and that her parents had not survived the accident.

She had grown up moving from place to place, asking for alms. Sometimes, if she was lucky, people gave her some clothes and food. She didn't know what love and affection meant and had lost all hope of a better life. She would often break down, thinking of her pitiful plight, and today was another such day.

She silently observed the people celebrating around her. She thought miserably about all the other children who had nice, cosy houses. How lucky they were to know where their next meal would be coming from! And just then, as though an angel had read her thoughts, a couple came over and gave her a small box of sweets. The lady beamed at her with a dimpled smile and the man looked at her kindly through his rimmed glasses. She had never felt so warm before and the little orphan thanked them from the bottom of her heart.

'My heart bleeds for that girl,' said Radhika, the lady who had given the girl the sweets. 'Yes, dear, but we did brighten her day,' responded her husband Raj. They walked by all the well-lit shops, decorated for Diwali, in silence till they reached their house. It was a duplex building with a large garden in the front, with colourful flowers and lush green grass. Radhika went up to her room quietly as Raj made himself comfortable on the sofa. He opened his laptop to continue working on his latest project. He was an architect and Radhika was a freelance writer and novelist.

Right now, Radhika was thinking about the poor girl she had seen on the streets. She and Raj had been married for over twelve years and they had no children. She had always wanted a child and although Raj never spoke about it, she knew very well that he secretly hoped for a child too. An idea formed at the back of her mind and the next day, after Raj left for work, she went outside. She walked down the street to the place where she had seen the girl the previous evening. The girl was asleep. Radhika admired the girl's angelic face for a while as she slept. She had brought a parcel with her and carefully, she placed it next to the girl and walked back home.

The girl woke up after an hour or so and was surprised to see a parcel wrapped in brown paper next to her. She quickly opened it and found a few chocolates and a small doll in it. She was stunned but had no idea who had kept them there. She looked at the doll again; she had seen it in a few shops this season. She had to keep telling herself that this

was not a dream and that it was indeed actually happening!

Slowly, this became a routine. The girl kept getting happier day by day. Finally, after a week, Radhika decided to tell the girl that it was she who was her secret angel. The girl started crying when Radhika finally revealed her little secret. Radhika smiled, hugged the girl and fed her the cakes she had brought for her that day. 'Thank you!' said the girl as Radhika waved goodbye and walked back to her house.

In the evening, when Raj was back after a long day's work, Radhika told him what she had done in the morning. 'Why did you do that?' he asked.

'I think the girl needs to get used to being pampered,' smiled Radhika.

'What do you mean?' Raj was baffled. Radhika explained that she had thought of adopting the girl and asked Raj if he was with her. Raj thought for a very long time and after what seemed like a decade, he finally nodded. Radhika had known that her dear husband could not resist the idea of having a child in the house.

The next day, the sun rose as usual, but for Radhika and Raj, it was a whole new beginning. They walked up together to the girl. Three hearts beat at an amazing rate as Raj explained to the girl that she now had a new home, a new life and a new world ahead of her. She could barely believe her ears. They quietly shared a moment of immense pleasure. Then they walked hand in hand, away from their old lives to a new world: a world where prayers did come true!

if i could talk to animals

Trusha Ganesh, Age: 12, Goa

Just before thirteen-year-old Indigo Bleu could twist the knob of the door that led to her room, she heard something scuttling behind her. 'Who goes there?' she demanded, her face turning pale, just before she spotted the shaggy mane of her pet dog Tyson. 'Oh, it's only you, darling,' she said, heaving a sigh of relief.

'You really do need to get those books dusted,' her puppy observed, enthusiastically wagging his tail. Indigo froze.

'You…you spoke?' she asked, her legs trembling.

'Surprised me too,' her dog replied, inching towards her.

Indigo was going to scream out her mother's name in fright when her cocker spaniel put his petite paws against his snout and said, 'Shush, Indigo! I'm not going to hurt you.'

Indigo gathered her wits and tried to breathe calmly, trying to take in the fact that her dog had just conversed with her.

'Don't be afraid, I don't want to hurt you,' Tyson reassured her. 'Come sit down,' he suggested, patting the bean bag that was lying on the carpeted floor before him. Indigo nodded, and flopped on to the seat that her pup had gestured towards. Then she realized that Tyson was looking at her expectantly, as if waiting for her to say something. She racked her brains for a suitable response.

'Umm…what is it like? Being you, I mean,' she asked finally.

'Oh, it's terrible,' Tyson said with an exaggerated shudder. 'To answer your question in more detail, let me take you through a typical day in the life of Tyson Bleu.'

Indigo clasped her hands around her knees in anticipation.

'Well, it starts when Mum ushers me out of my cosy duvet at around eight in the morning. I beg for a few extra minutes of slumber, but my pleas falls on deaf ears. So I trot down the stairs and give you a parting lick before that beast of a school bus snatches you away from me for the rest of the day. I spend the next couple of hours following Mum around the house. As soon as the grandfather clock chimes half-past twelve, I begin to subtly remind Mum about my midday meal. Roughly about fifteen minutes later, Mum bustles into the kitchen and prepares a steaming lunch for me. I relish every morsel.' Here Tyson smacked his tongue.

'Well, after my bowl of kibble, I curl up in the master bedroom for a siesta. I dream about ice cream and chew toys and a slim waistline. Dad interrupts my snooze in a few hours. After a feeble protest, I patiently await your arrival. As soon as the school bus halts in front of the yard, I march up to you and give you a royal welcome.

'Once you have entered your study, I know that you will not emerge till twilight sets in. So I find a suitable nook where I nap a little more. What can I say? I need my twenty-two hours of beauty sleep! Anyway, once you reappear from the dreaded study, you set off for dinner. I, like your devoted buddy, flop on to your feet and don't budge till you've wiped the last crumb off the plate. As soon as the family has dined, Mum serves me my dinner, which I happily polish off. After slurping up my last snack of the day, I follow you to your room before slumping down in my basket beside your four-poster bed.

'Thus ends a satisfactory day in the life of Tyson Bleu, a workaholic, who never rests for a moment,' Tyson groaned dramatically to which Indigo could only smile.

five thousand rupees

Arundhati Mukherjee, Age: 15, Kolkata

The perfect family holiday would be one where you were away from all kinds of worry and distraction, where you could just sit back and relax. However, this is seldom the case. There is bound to be something or the other that causes anxiety and worry. As for distractions, the mobile phone, of course, serves the purpose. In spite of this, we must get on with the story which is, as you might have guessed, about a family holiday.

The Mukherjees rarely ever went on a vacation. It was one of those rare occasions when they were on a five-day holiday to Siliguri. Siliguri would be the last destination a family would choose for a vacation. And yet here they were, all four of them: husband and wife and their two daughters. One of them was just a year shy of sixteen and the other was about eight years of age. The Mukherjees were staying at a plush resort, with all the modern amenities that one would require for recreation and rejuvenation. The resort had a pool and it was here by the poolside that the family was spending their evening. Mrs Mukherjee was toying with her newly-acquired mobile phone, a gift from her doting husband on their anniversary. Mr Mukherjee was lolling on the wicker chair, his corpulent body spilling out of it. The two daughters were bickering between themselves over some trivial matter. Just then, the waiter came in with the bill to interrupt this blissful family scene.

'Sir?'

'Yes?' came the curt reply from Mr Mukherjee.

'Your bill,' the waiter placed the bill on the glass table.

Mr Mukherjee languidly rose from his seat and looked at the nondescript bill and said, 'Include it with the rest of our bills. We will clear it all during checkout.'

The docile waiter nodded and took the bill away. In the meanwhile, the family got up to leave. Their luggage was waiting for them in the lobby and their car had arrived. Slowly but surely, they made their way to the lobby area and soon left in their car.

The waiter came back to clear the table and to his delight, he saw something lying on the table. It was Mrs Mukherjee's new mobile phone. His first impulse was to return it to the concierge but, on second thoughts, he shook himself out of the idea. First, they had not bothered to pay him a tip, second, his family was in deep penury and last, the Mukherjees were affluent enough to purchase another handset if they wished to. Assuring his conscience with these thoughts, the waiter quietly slipped the phone into his pocket.

Let us leave the waiter to his new-found fortune and take a look at the Mukherjee family. The four of them were waiting for their plane in the lounge of the Bagdogra airport. Mr Mukherjee was busy emailing his yearly review to his superiors while Mrs Mukherjee was busy looking over all the other people at the airport condescendingly. The two daughters were, as usual, endlessly bickering. All of a sudden, a shrill cry escaped the wife's lips, making all the others around her glare at her. Her husband asked, in an extremely indignant tone, 'What on earth has happened to you now?'

'My phone… It's gone…' Mrs Mukherjee's voice trailed off.

'What? You lost your mobile phone?' Mr Mukherjee said in a hollow whisper.

In the minutes that followed, the peace of the family went missing too. They searched every nook and cranny in the lounge but to no avail. The phone was nowhere to be found. The peaceful and happy family holiday had been reduced to a bitter memory, all because of the absconding phone. After turning all their belongings inside-out, Mr Mukherjee had a brainwave. Maybe his wife had left the phone at the resort. Without further ado, he immediately called up the manager of the resort. Unfortunately he could not help them either. The phone was lost. Forever.

Meanwhile, the waiter had gone to the nearest mobile phone dealer in town, who also happened to be a very close acquaintance of his. After a lot of haggling, the two friends reached a deal. The dealer offered him five thousand rupees for it, which was enough to sustain the waiter's seven children and wife at home. With a heart full of joy, he made his way home. But as he rushed to cross the road, he failed to see the truck that was coming towards him at full speed. For a moment, there was terror written all over his face before everything collapsed into darkness.

His children and wife were all eagerly waiting for his arrival home after a hard day's work. The wife was lovingly rolling out chapattis, beads of perspiration on her brow. The children were playing a game of hopscotch outside their humble house. The dealer, the harbinger of the unfortunate news, arrived at their doorstep. He was a picture of melancholy. The wife welcomed her husband's friend with earnestness. He refused to come in and mumbled, 'Your husband is dead.' She suddenly became cold and still like stone; he pulled her palm towards himself and placed in her hand the five thousand rupees that her husband had refused to part with, even in death; his blood-stained corpse had clutched it in its palm. But no amount of money or wealth could fill the void that was left in the family; the wife mourned the husband who would now be missing from their lives forever.

The Mukherjee family reached Kolkata safely and the first thing Mr Mukherjee did was to buy his wife a new phone. A cheaper one this time, one that cost only five thousand rupees.

the mysterious symbol

Pratiti Banerjee, Age: 13, Kolkata

It was the happiest day of my life. My little sister had been born. Well, she was crying at that moment, but I hoped it wouldn't be the daily routine for years to come! My parents and I had arranged a room for her where she would, no doubt, devise plans to annoy me when she got a little older. But this isn't where my story starts. Let's fast forward ten years to the present…

'Tinki, Tinki!'

'What, Mum?'

'Where is that incompetent sister of yours?'

Yes, this is our family scenario ten years after Pinki, my sister, was born. She is a little mysterious, as all her teachers say. She either doesn't have food for days or gobbles up as many as seventeen chapattis in one sitting; she either fails a second grade maths test or solves graduate-level sums; she either sulks for a week or constantly talks non-stop. She shows interest in Egyptology and Astrophysics, not subjects that ten year olds usually like. Her only age-appropriate hobby is drawing.

One fine summer day, my parents have gone out for a seminar and Pinki and I are alone. Pinki goes to her room and starts drawing on a huge sheet of paper.

'What are you drawing, Pinki?'

No answer.

'Pinks? Everything okay, sis?'

Still no answer.

I assume she is in her I-will-not-talk-for-a-week mode and make a beeline for my room.

The phone rings. 'Hey Tinki!' It's my friend Devi. 'Are you busy?'

'No. Mum and Dad are not here. Pinki and I are alone.'

'That's great! The other day, when I was in the library, I found a quaint looking book with a capsule inside. I took it home.'

'Carry on.'

'I left the capsule on the table and when I came back I saw it had cracked and there was a piece of paper inside. It was a map to a lime kiln, which is now the pastry shop near school. What do you think? You want to check it out?'

'Sounds great! How about around ten?'

'Done.'

So I leave Pinki at home and take with me a knapsack with a torch, a packet of biscuits, a knife and a cellphone inside. I meet Devi at the pastry shop at ten o'clock. She has her capsule and the piece of paper. We begin exploring.

We first go to the locked door at a corner of the pastry shop. I pick the lock with my knife. It's a pretty old lock, and it opens quite easily. I light my torch and we go inside. We find a lot of things: a pair of freshly-polished shoes, a weird looking hat, a bathrobe-type robe, a dog and a piece of parchment that says:

'All Pigmalites, the third world Pigmalite Annual Conference will take place on the fifth Sunday of Pigmamonth. As you know, the Pigmamonth festivities include the slaying of a dog, the ceremonial offering of the Pigmarobe, and the dance of the tri-world leaders.

P.S.: The newly elected president is Pinki Banerjee from Earth.'

What I should've said was, 'Oh no! My sister is the president of an alien club! What will my parents, friends and relatives say? I am ruined!'

Instead, what I say is, 'I knew it! All those drawings were for this club. All those weird symbols that she drew were for the club's logo. Oh God, how could I have not known all this while?'

But wait a second, where's Devi? 'DEVI?' I scream.

There is a short, stout, weird-looking creature standing where my friend was standing a second ago. It has a mysterious symbol on its forehead. Oh no! Devi, too, is a Pigmalite! I run in the opposite direction when I see a glowing being coming towards me. She has the same symbol on her forehead. I conclude that the symbol is the source of the Pigmalites' power. Suddenly, I recognize the glowing being. It is my *sister*, and she is coming closer and closer and closer...

'Tinki! Get up right now! Your dad and I are going out. Take care of your sister!'

I get up sleepily. Was it all a dream? I look around for my knapsack but it isn't there. I check on Pinki. She is drawing... it's the same symbol I saw in my dream. I find a piece of parchment on my table: the Pigmaclub invite. I call Devi.

'Hello, Devi?'

'Oh my God, Tinki! You won't believe the dream I had last night...'

when i aimed right

Shah Kashish, Age: 14, Ahmedabad

During those days, I was desperate to earn money. I had never seen my mother's face and had grown up in an orphanage. I was brought there by an elderly man who found me as a baby, lying in a basket on a deserted street. At fifteen, I left the orphanage and started working at a city mall. But the job was poorly paid and it became difficult for me to make a living. I was forever looking for an opportunity to earn money and I finally got it.

One fine morning, when I was cleaning the glass windows of the mall, I spotted a notice announcing that an archery competition was to be held in the city. The winner would be awarded a cash prize of fifty thousand rupees. The amount was equivalent to my annual salary. I had been fond of archery from childhood and was a good archer. I even possessed a set of bow and arrows. So I decided to register my name for the competition.

I started practising after my duty hours. I chose an empty soft drink can as my target and started aiming for it with the arrow. Initially I missed the target but afterwards my hands steadied and I achieved perfection in hitting the target. I had decided to not let this chance go. I practised harder than ever.

Finally the day arrived. The sun rose, filling me with confidence and positive energy. I set off towards the Vishwanath grounds, where the event was being held. The seats were packed with people cheering and roaring. Over five thousand people had gathered to witness the competition.

A man in a blue uniform announced the start of the competition. The archers took their positions with the circular rings, their targets, in front of them, ten metres away. It was the qualifying round. The competition was divided in four parts. With each round, the distance between the archers and their target was increased by five metres. I focused and shot the arrow. To my pleasure and surprise, it went straight into the innermost black ring. This perfect aim boosted my confidence. My grip on the bow relaxed. I passed the next two rounds with ease and the audience started cheering me, shouting, clapping and enjoying themselves.

I entered the final round with a performance above par. Now I looked around to the other competitors and saw, to my surprise, that the other finalist was none other than my neighbour, Shambhu. He lived near my house and ran a general store.

He shot the arrow first and it hit just outside the innermost black circle. Then it was my turn. I pulled the string of the bow with the arrow in between my thumb and my forefinger, took aim and released the arrow. It remained in air for twenty-five meters and hit the outermost ring. The audience was shocked. They could not believe their eyes. How could a person who had performed so consistently throughout the day have missed the target? I did not wait after this. I just ran towards the exit, looking down at the ground.

That evening, Shambhu came to my house with his eight-year-old daughter and said, 'Thank you, thank you very much. You missed on purpose. You knew...' He could not speak further. He was crying and so was his sweet daughter. He handed me a new set of bow and arrows and left. After he

went away, I thanked God that at least I could see the world around me. Shambhu's daughter was blind. He needed the money for her treatment.

Even today, my condition has not improved. But I do not regret my decision. Shambhu's daughter got her sight back and can now play with other children. So what if I could not achieve my dream, did I not become a hero in the eyes of Shambhu and his family?

home alone

Adarsh Menon, Age: 10, Greater Noida

I was five years old. I had woken up unusually early. A nightmare had woken me up. I lay back on my bed and tried to sleep. But I couldn't. I kept thinking about how, in my dream, my house had been haunted by scary, yucky things.

I finally got up with a groan. I called out for my mother and father but no one replied. I was scared out of my wits. I searched the house but I couldn't find anyone. I remembered that I had had a fight with them yesterday over whether I should get a game or not. But it was more of a debate, I thought. Why would someone leave their family if they lost a debate? How cowardly of them to leave me!

I went to the door to go out, but, even when I pushed with all my might, the door wouldn't budge. I asked politely, 'Please could you open up, Mr Door?' but Mr Door was adamant. Maybe I'll teach him manners later, I thought, like they taught me in school. My stomach was grumbling so I went to the kitchen. I knew I was not allowed to, but, in situations concerning life or death, you have to take decisions like that. I didn't know where any of the stuff was kept, so I had to explore each one of the shelves. I never knew that it was dangerous until the tin of sugar fell on my head. The next second, there was a lump on my head.

I thought of calling the police. In school they had taught us to dial '100' in case of an emergency. I thought of charging my parents of abandonment, but that, I thought, would be

too rude. I tried the door again but it still hadn't changed its mind. I looked at the time, it was seventy-thirty in the morning. I thought of escaping by jumping out the windows, as I had seen people do in movies. The problem was that I couldn't reach the windows.

Now, this was freaking me out. I realized I was home alone. I started regretting the debate about the game. I went to my room. I realized I hadn't brushed, because Mommy generally did it for me. I wasn't in the habit of brushing myself, because I had heard that too much physical activity was not good for the human body. I started playing with my toys. But after some time, I became extremely bored. I took it out on a stuffed teddy bear. I was going to shower my wrath on another stuffed toy—a dog—but it was too cute, so I let it go. I thought of drawing something, but I dropped it after I realized I couldn't draw much. I thought about the lump on my head. It was burning. I ran cold water over it, and the pain slowly receded. I looked at the time again: ten o'clock. It was time for my favourite cartoon: *Timon and Pumbaa*. I watched till eleven until there was a powercut. The power came back in half an hour and I sat under the fan to get rid of the sweat. I was very sticky.

Suddenly I heard a noise from the door. And lo, it was my parents, but with someone new with them! My mother told me that she had had a big tummy because she had been pregnant and that she went into labour in the dead of the night and that I have a baby sister now and blah blah blah, but I was just happy that she was finally back.

candyfloss

Leena Gupta, Age: 15, Kolkata

The centre aisle of the train was filled with people standing elbow to elbow. The man in front of her smelled of cigarettes and roasted chicken. Every few minutes, wafts of cheap perfume would reach her nose from an unknown place. The beads of sweat on her forehead had multiplied, owing to the rise in temperature or pressure or humidity—she couldn't remember which one, although she had heard her sister talking about it only this morning. The train was nearing the stop where she was to get down. Her heart was pounding with excitement. She was suddenly nervous. She ran her fingers through her hair, but it was more entangled than ever.

After five seconds, the train screeched to a halt and people went pouring out of the gates. She stepped out on to the platform. In front of her was a huge board, yellow in colour, which read, 'Welcome to Ballygunge Station'. She adjusted her bag on her shoulders but the new Fastrack bag slipped and fell on the dusty platform. She picked it up quickly. She searched for the exit gate but couldn't find one, although she had made innumerable train trips through this station. After fifteen more minutes, she finally found the gate marked 'EXIT' on her left. There was a strange twinkle in her eyes that were searching for Ranbir and her mouth had unknowingly curved into a smile.

She stepped out into the busy street lined with vendors. The September sun felt delicious on her skin and the sweet smell of roses and jasmines at the flowerseller's was diffused in the atmosphere.

'Ragini!'

She heard someone call her name from behind. Ragini Oberoi turned around. She looked like any other twenty-five-year-old girl, with shoulder length black hair and chocolate brown eyes but the Monalisa-like mystifying grin on her face made her a bit different from other girls her age. Ragini turned around, but the smile on her face vanished when she saw who had called out to her. It was her cousin, Neeraj. She started running. She ran and ran until she reached a garbage heap and hid behind it. She hated the idea of having to face Neeraj. She hated him for taking her to some psychiatrist every second day who continuously asked her questions about her personal life and said awful things about Ranbir. How senseless and cruel! But Ragini hated Neeraj even more these days because she had heard him saying that she should be sent to a rehabilitation centre. She didn't want to go anywhere without Ranbir and so, she had decided to run away with him to some distant place, away from her family and Neeraj. They said she had a strange disease whose name she did not remember. Last night, she had sent a message to Ranbir's mobile saying, 'Ranbir, my family wants to send me far away. In spite of our engagement, they don't allow me to go out alone, even when I say I want to meet you. Please save me. Meet me tomorrow at the airport and I will run away with you. Buy tickets for the Indigo 5236 (Kolkata-Dubai) flight and board the plane. I'll be there. Bye...' But she didn't notice the service reply: 'Not delivered. Number does not exist.'

Right now, she only concentrated on hiding behind the garbage heap and meeting Ranbir. But wait, where? Ragini couldn't remember where she had promised to meet Ranbir. She concentrated hard, and after almost an hour, Ragini remembered. She stepped out into the open again. It was past noon, she guessed. After walking up to the bus stand, waited for the Dumdum Airport bus and boarded it. In another hour, she reached the airport and went in. Purchasing the tickets for Indigo 5236, she decided to have a burger. Although she had been here barely a month ago, she couldn't find the McDonald's. Strange, she thought again. All of a sudden, she saw a sweet shop. She rushed in there and bought her favourite pink candyfloss. Candyfloss was the one thing that both Ragini and Ranbir had loved. She smiled at the thought. She went strolling in the lobby of the airport but froze midway when she saw Neeraj again, this time with a man dressed in a khaki uniform. In sudden panic, she put the candyfloss in her bag and ran to the ladies' washroom. The flight was to leave in an hour. Ragini managed to sneak out through the back door of the washroom after a long time. She went to her terminal just when the flight was about to leave. She took her seat panting and turned around to search for Ranbir. On the last seat, a fair complexioned man with spiked hair and spectacles smiled at her. Ragini smiled back and immediately fell asleep, without having her dinner or her candyfloss.

In the morning, when she woke up, Ranbir was nowhere to be found. The flight was to land in another fifteen minutes. She showed Ranbir's photo to her co-passengers, but they denied having seen him. Ragini cried endlessly. At the Dubai airport, she began searching for him again, in the hope that Ranbir was only playing a prank, but all in vain. The candyfloss in her bag had turned into a solid mass by then, but it didn't

TY CLOTHSTE

matter to her any more. In the Dubai airport, Neeraj found Ragini and took her back to Kolkata, not saying a word throughout the journey. Back in Kolkata, she resumed her daily routine of seeing psychiatrists.

The candyfloss in her bag lay uneaten. She swore she would eat it only with Ranbir. Then one day, Ragini opened her bag only to find her leftover money and a pink note saying,

'The candyfloss is mine this time <3.'

Tears swelled in her eyes. 'I was always right. Ranbir is still there. I don't know what happened. But he still loves me and I know that. Let the psychiatrists say that he is no more. It's just a bad dream, nothing else.' Outside the room, Neeraj was in tears. He knew he hadn't done the right thing as a brother, but he was helpless. He couldn't see Ragini like that. On the flight, Ragini had seen nothing but a hallucination of Ranbir, her fiancé—the man who had died in a car accident the day after their engagement. But how could they make her believe this? What if she ran away again? She had done so five times already. Neeraj closed his eyes and sighed.

After ten years, Ragini's Alzheimer's disease was treated by regular medication and a three-year stay at the rehabilitation centre. The memories of Ranbir had been completely erased from her mind. But she always felt an eerie sense of panic whenever she saw pink candyfloss. However hard she concentrated, she couldn't come up with the reason, and only the smell of sweet roses and jasmines clung to her mind.

a very special friend

Tanishaa Sinha, Age: 9, New Delhi

In the outskirts of the city, there was a dense forest. All you could hear there was the hissing of the wind and the sound of fallen leaves—a sound that could make your hair stand on end. But this was not so with Mohan, a poor boy who had come into the forest to pick wood for a fire. He heard a sound and stood motionless. Something or someone was approaching him and he waited for it. There was no one around to help. Mohan waited with bated breath. Finally, he saw a pair of shining bright eyes approaching him. Now Mohan was very scared and he fainted.

After some time, he felt a tickle and tried to open his eyes. He could feel the fresh air around him and the sun on him through the trees. As he regained consciousness, he was amazed at what he saw! Beside him stood a beautiful deer with sparkling eyes. Its eyes appeared to be filled with pure innocence, love and wisdom.

Mohan got up. He looked at the deer and was drawn towards it. He touched her. She licked him. They played for a long time. Soon Mohan realized it was late. He picked up the logs and went home happily. He told his parents about Sundari. Yes! He had named his new friend Sundari, as she was so beautiful. His parents were happy that he had at last found a friend. Mohan had never had the joy of having friends. He had had polio as a child. It made him limp. All the children around him made fun of him and would not play with him. Today, after ten years, he had finally found a

friend! His joy knew no bounds. He went to bed and could not wait to meet Sundari again.

The next morning, he woke up early, finished all his chores and went to meet Sundari again. He found her standing under a tree. They had a lovely time. Sundari also introduced Mohan to some of her animal friends. All of them became his friends but Sundari was his best friend. He knew she could not talk but looking at her, he sometimes felt that Sundari was talking to him. The animals were better than human friends and Mohan was thankful to God for that. They played every day in the jungle.

One day, some children were playing nearby. They saw Mohan with Sundari and the other animals. They were astonished at how easily Mohan mingled with the animals and how much fun they seemed to be having. One boy asked, 'Will you and your friends play with us?' Sundari licked Mohan and he said 'Sure.' Soon, the other children were also having a good time playing with the animals and Mohan.

The next day, when Mohan reached the forest, he heard the sound of gunshots. He was terrified. He went to look for Sundari and his other animal friends. He knew there was a hunter there. The hunter heard his footsteps and mistook him for an animal and shot again. Before the bullet reached Mohan, Sundari jumped out in front of him from nowhere. She got shot instead of Mohan. She went to sleep forever. Mohan, all the other animals and the children were devastated. The hunter also repented when he heard Mohan's story and how Sundari had saved him. He decided to never hunt again.

Sundari was gone forever. But she had given Mohan a lifetime of happiness and friends. Sundari had been a true friend indeed.

shipwrecked with shahrukh khan

Vrinda Sood, Age: 15, New Delhi

'AAAAAAHHHHHH!'

I screamed as I stared at the unending blue of the Pacific Ocean. My mother would tease that I was preparing to survive a shipwreck when she saw me watching the nail-biting episodes of the TV series *Lost*.

Damn coincidences.

I had been stuck on this godforsaken island for the past forty-five minutes, and it was beginning to bug me now. Quite literally, I thought, as I brushed off a small slimy insect from my thigh. How did I even end up here, I asked myself for the twentieth time. And I was reminded of my folly.

Two hours earlier

'DADDY! NO!' I screamed as he tilted me further towards the edge of the ship. I was on a Pacific Ocean cruise with my entire family. It had been three days, and apart from entertaining my highly irritating younger cousins and (in Daddy's words) 'soaking in the beauty of our surroundings', I hadn't had much to do. My mother had been pestering me to accompany her to the on-cruise pilates class, but just reading their tagline, 'Say no to fat! Say yes to bikinis!' and the thought of being in a roomful of fat arm-flapping aunties

was enough to make me turn on my heels and run.

So my father was stuck with me complaining day in and day out about how he was letting me waste my youth by not making me do anything exciting.

I was so persistent that at the end of the third day, he picked me up, threw me over his shoulder (I am fairly light) and proceeded to carry me over to the edge of the ship.

'So you want adventure, huh?' he asked calmly.

'Finally! Yes!' I said, excited.

'Well, how's this for adventure?' he said, tilting me upside down over the rim of the ship, with a firm grip on my waist.

My eyes widened, and I screamed, 'No, Daddy! Put me down!'

He laughed, setting me down. 'Tch. Tch. And here I thought you weren't a whimpering little sissy girl.'

'Is that what you think I am?' I asked, annoyed.

'Well, of course. You should have heard yourself yelping,' he said, chuckling to himself.

'I'll prove you wrong,' I said, tears stinging my eyes.

'Well, you could,' he mused, 'but you might break a nail.'

With a hurt ego, I decided that I *had* to prove him wrong. I looked all around and, spotting a life boat, I proceeded to haul it down. I wasn't thinking about anything but the fact that I had to prove my father wrong.

I threw it into the water, and following suit, I looked back and screamed, 'See you on the other side!'

The only thing I remember is looking into my father's widened, slightly baffled eyes—as if his brain had not yet fully processed what had happened. After that, all I remember is turbulence, and finally, stumbling on to this island.

◆

My stomach growled. In the distance, the sun was setting. I realized that the last thing I had eaten was the brochettes gambas in the cruise buffet, which was just a fancy name for skewered shrimp. It was as disgusting to eat as it was hard to pronounce. Yet I was dying for some right now. Something, anything.

I forced myself to get up and scavenge for food. I had walked around the whole island once, right after I stumbled on to it, and it was fairly small, with a forest lining it at one end. I had been too scared to go into the forest earlier, but now I realized I had to. After I get back home, I really need to re-evaluate how I make big life decisions, I thought to myself as I walked towards the forest. I looked back once, wondering if I would ever see the water again. I had done everything I had seen in the first few episodes of *Lost*: make a help sign, rationed my supplies (after which I had found out that I had no food or water) and even written an epitaph for myself. It read: 'R.I.P. Vrinda Sood, the girl who defied the laws of common sense.'

Walking through the pitch dark forest, with my only companions my flashlight and the crunching sound of the soil beneath my feet, I suddenly came to a halt. Lying in front of me was a shiny red backpack. It looked like it had been abandoned by a traveller.

'Praise the Lord!' I exclaimed as I grabbed it, unzipping it, not being able to believe my luck. Inside, I found a pack of three chocolate bars, a keychain and a whole lot of small, colourful bits of paper.

'Confetti?' I wondered aloud, as I pulled out fistful after

fistful of that stuff. It made me wonder if a four-year-old had packed that bag. To my utter dismay, I found there was no water.

Rushing back to the beach, I sat down and hungrily took out the chocolates. After I had wolfed them down in about ten seconds flat, I lay down with a contented smile on my face. Maybe this wasn't that bad after all, I thought, as I drifted off to sleep, the cool breeze tickling my nose.

I was woken up rudely by my own subconscious. I suddenly sat up straight, my eyes wide, only to be forced to squint because the blazing sun was right above my head. My clothes were soaked, I was drenched in sweat, but my throat was parched. I had been without water for more than twenty-four hours now.

I heard a whistle towards my left. There, lying bronzed in the sun like a timeless statue of a Greek god, was none other than Shahrukh Khan. I couldn't believe my eyes! The man I had drooled over since I could understand the concept of movies was right in front of me.

I approached him carefully, and he motioned me to sit right next to him.

Maintaining a reasonable distance, I sat down to his left.

He opened his mouth, as if to say something, but instead just pointed towards the far east.

I looked to my left, overwhelmed by curiosity, finding nothing but the waves splashing against the shore. I looked back, about to ask Shahrukh what he meant, only to find an empty space next to me.

I raised my eyebrows and sat gaping, asking myself where he had gone, where he had come from, and what he had been doing here. And then I understood what had happened.

So deprived of water was I that I had… started hallucinating. I had started imagining cheesy Hindi film heroes. Great, I was going crazy.

Overwhelmed by the situation and the thought of madness descending over me, I did what only the bravest can do. I cried. Burying my head in my hands, convinced that my end had come, I let my tears flow shamelessly. People think holding on to hope is something that kids are good at. But it's hard. It's very, very hard.

After what seemed like hours, my crying was interrupted by a loud 'tak tak tak tak' sound coming from the sky.

I glanced upwards, welcoming what I thought would be the cause of my death, only to see a large helicopter. With the last shred of hope in my heart giving me an ounce of energy, I leapt up, screaming and waving my hands. It started approaching the island, and not knowing what to do, I just hugged myself with happiness. As it neared, I saw a tall man hanging from the side, and I smiled to myself.

'DADDY!' I screamed, running towards him. He was here for me! He had come to save me!

As soon as the helicopter landed, he jumped off and started walking towards me, a look of relief on his face.

'You, young lady, are grounded for life!' he said, picking me up in his arms. I didn't care. He could punish me any way he wanted, I was just glad to have him back. We were hurried on to the chopper and as it took off, I gulped down water from a bottle, sighing loudly with relief. My father said, 'Well, you did prove me wrong. It must have been one hell of an adventure.'

'Oh it was,' I said, beaming to myself.

the gift

Saranya Das Sharma, Age: 13, New Delhi

It was a sunny morning. I could hear birds singing outside my window. The sun filtered in through the curtains, casting an orangish glow around my room. I yawned happily and looked at my alarm clock. My eyes popped out! It was nine-thirty already and school started at nine!

It wasn't any ordinary school day either. It was my first day at my new school, where I was on a full scholarship. I was very excited as I was studying two of my favourite subjects here—drama and writing, along with other subjects. The school was very strict. What if they revoked my scholarship?

I put my head down and began to cry. I wished I could rewind time. I wished it was only eight! Suddenly, the room started spinning. Maybe I was hallucinating because of my state. I tried to calm myself down and took a deep breath.

Just then, I heard the loud beep of my alarm clock. I looked at the clock and was aghast! It said eight a.m.! That was impossible. Then I heard the chugging of a train. Its whistle pierced the peaceful morning. This was the morning train! I rubbed my eyes and went to the window. It was the same train, the green and red one with a golden stripe in the middle—the one I called the Christmas Present—that passed by my window every morning at eight o'clock. I could not believe what had just happened. I had turned back time! I grinned widely.

This was amazing. But I needed to know why. I didn't

want to ask my parents, they would tell me not to make things up. The only person I could ask was my grandfather. I had just enough time to call him.

'Hello,' he said, picking up the phone.

'Hi, Grandpa. I have something to tell you,' I said, explaining the situation.

'My grandmother could play with time, too,' he said after hearing me. 'She had told us that once in every four generations someone in the family has this gift. You are the fourth generation. She has left a letter for you. I'll give it to you when I come and pick you up after school,' he said.

I thanked him and told my parents that I would be late because I was going to my grandparents' house after school.

That day at school all I could do was wait for the day to end so I could read that letter.

Finally, I went to my grandparents' house after school. After a hurried snack, Grandpa handed me an envelope. In it was a letter, yellowed with time. It said, 'Travel to Fern Estate, Shimla, in the year 1930 and then go to the Great Hall.' I looked at my grandfather and asked him what it meant.

'Read the instructions,' he advised. The instructions told me to think of the time and place I wanted to go to and said that I would reach that place and time.

◆

I found myself in a large bungalow. It was cool and light filtered in through a small skylight. There was a mahogany table opposite the door, which a man was dusting.

'Excuse me, I need to go to the Great Hall,' I said.

'The Great Hall is opposite the garden. It is a large marble building. Madam does her work there,' the man said. 'And

may I enquire about the purpose of your visit?'

'I'm not sure myself,' I said.

'Please, go ahead,' he said.

I walked down through the passage, my shoes clicking on the marble. I passed a beautiful garden, exploding with the colours of the different varieties of flowers growing there. At the end of the garden was the hall.

At the entrance of the hall stood a woman wearing a blue salwar kameez. She was old. The sun reflected off her silver hair. She looked up at me, her smile lines showing.

'My name is Saranya. I'm your great-great granddaughter. I can turn time,' I said. She smiled.

'Come, let me give you a hug. I'm afraid I don't have time to chat. I am very busy,' she said, hugging me.

'What are you doing?' I asked.

'I am on the last part of my breakthrough in translating the language Rongorongo,' she said, smiling and scribbling notes.

'Rongorongo? But that's not possible. It's still undiscovered,' I said. Rongorongo had been found on tablets in the Easter Islands. The Peruvians had killed all the wise men on the island so nobody knew how to read it. I had learnt about it in school.

'Translating these tablets have been my life's work,' she paused for a moment, wrote something else and smiled, 'and I have just finished it.'

'That's amazing! But then, why doesn't the world know?' I asked, flummoxed.

'I'm unsure,' she mused, 'perhaps I died before it was unveiled to the world. You cannot alter history but you can finish my work. Take this manuscript and show it to the world. It will unravel many mysteries.'

Before I knew it, I was standing in my grandparents' house, clutching the manuscript. I could hear my great-great grandmother's voice in my head.

'Be successful and happy. Remember to use your gift wisely,' she told me. I realized that I had returned with not one but two gifts—the precious manuscript and the ability to play with time.

I looked up and said, 'Don't worry great-great Grandma, I'll use both wisely.'

memories never die

Shramona Roy, Age: 14, Pune

It is said that memories never die. We have all heard this line countless times. However, seldom do we realize the depth of this phrase. In our busy, hectic lives, we tend to forget what happened only two minutes ago, so trying to remember what happened in our childhood is not something we usually do. I was no exception, until the day I, quite accidentally, came across an old photo album.

The whole house was in a mess. We were relocating because of my dad's transfer. Most of the furniture had already been sent ahead of us. What was left was my old childhood trunk. It had been almost a decade since I had last opened it and a thick layer of dust had accumulated on it. As I opened it, a musty smell filled the air. Slightly reluctant, I began sifting through the contents—my playroom kitchen set, discarded Barbie dolls, picture books and a photo album.

I do not know what came over me. Before I realized it, I was sitting down and gazing at the first picture. It had my grandmother sitting in a wheelchair and a tiny me standing beside her. As soon as I set my eyes on it, a wave of memories rushed over me. It was as if a curtain had been lifted and I was back to my childhood. I began to remember...

My grandmother was my best friend in those years. Even though she had arthritis and was confined to a wheelchair, she was still, in my opinion, the liveliest person in the family. My mother was often busy with her household chores and so for the better part of the day, I used to be with my grandmother.

Sometimes my grandmother would make me sit beside her on her bed and I would go on and on with my childish gibberish. She would then become my patient and I the doctor, she my daughter and I her mother and such games would go on throughout the day. I would sit with rapt attention as she narrated to me stories of faraway princesses locked away by an ugly demon or of the two princes lost in the desert. She never seemed to get tired of my non-stop chattering and bore it all with a patient and amused smile.

I remember that she had an uncanny ability to soothe me when I was agitated. There were countless times when someone had scolded me and I had taken refuge in her lap. She would listen patiently to my petty grievances and, with that fantastic ability of hers, pacify me. She was so good at it that before long I would again be smiling up at her, describing animatedly how Ma was cooking in the kitchen.

Then one day, when I was on a vacation with my parents, the news reached us that my grandmother had been taken ill at our Kolkata home. We immediately rushed back but we were too late. Her lifeless body was laid out in our drawing room. I was too small then to understand the gravity of the loss. I do not remember much of that day. I only remember that I had felt completely deserted.

I was so absorbed in my thoughts that I did not realize when a drop of tear trickled down my cheek. As I came back to reality, I swear I felt as if my grandmother was sitting on the bed, right beside me.

We relocated as per schedule, but throughout the journey the remembrance of that day, when I had discovered the photo album, kept coming back to me. It had been an unforgettable

experience. Truly, memories never die. Now, as our train hurled us towards the unknown, the truth of those words kept coming back to me. No matter how old we get or how busy we become, our memories always keep us true to ourselves.

Today, I am not sad that my grandmother left me at such a tender age. After that day's experience, I realize that those we truly love never really leave us. They are always there in our hearts, we only need to look inside us to find them again. They will forever be there to guide us and protect us. People may change, time may fly, but a memory lives on and never dies.

treasure island

Srishti Mitra, Age: 14, Pune

When I was small, I dreamt of sailing on the ocean. Chasing my childhood dream, I decided to become an explorer along with my friend Nisha.

Nisha and I combined our resources and bought a boat. It was quite small. It was meant for only two people, so it was perfect for us. It was our companion on all our journeys.

Once, when we were sailing across the Pacific Ocean, I went up on deck and saw a cloud bank rolling towards us.

'There's a storm coming, Nisha!' I yelled.

We tried to steer our boat away from it, but it eventually caught up with us. Nisha and I fought to keep the boat above water, but we were fighting a losing battle. Suddenly, a huge wave overturned our boat, and we were flung into the icy depths of the ocean.

The next thing I knew, I was lying on sand and Nisha was bending over me.

'What happened?' I asked. 'Where am I?'

'I have no clue either,' replied Nisha. 'But I was so scared! You weren't moving for half an hour.'

I got up and stared around me. We were on a beach that was surrounded by a forest on three sides.

'Are we on the mainland? Or is this an island?' I asked. Nisha shrugged.

'I think it's more likely to be an island,' she said. 'We were quite far out at sea when the storm hit.'

'How will we get away from here?' I asked.

'I have my radio transmitter in my pocket,' she said. 'It might still work.'

But when she took it out, all our hopes were shattered.

'The radio's fine,' she said. 'But the batteries are ruined.'

'We need something to eat and get our strength back before we do any exploring,' I said.

So Nisha and I ventured into the jungle. The canopy was quite thick and the few feeble rays of sunlight that filtered through made the jungle look even more dark and gloomy. We stumbled many a time on the thick creepers that snaked their way across the forest floor.

Many questions were going through my mind. I voiced some of them to Nisha.

'Do you think this place is inhabited?'

'No.'

'Have you seen this island before?'

'No.'

After a few more questions, I realized that Nisha was in no mood to talk. We trudged on in silence.

Suddenly, I came across some fruit trees.

'Nisha!' I said. 'Look, food!'

Nisha ran over to me. 'You idiot!' she said. 'Those are lemons. We can't eat them.'

'I'll still take some of them along,' I said, and stuffed a few in my pocket. We moved on.

We finally came out of the forest on the other side of the island. The beach here was much wider than the one we had landed on. However, I realized that there were jagged rocks off the coast. It would be a nightmare for sailors. As a confirmation of my thoughts, there was the wreck of an old

galleon to one side. It loomed over us.

'I don't like the look of that,' said Nisha uncomfortably.

'I'll explore this wreck and see if we can get anything useful out of it,' I said. I climbed up the side of the ship and stood on its deck.

The ship was old but it still had an air of grandeur about it. I tried to imagine what it would have been like long ago. Suddenly the rotten floorboards gave way and I found myself plunging through the deck into a small room below.

When I had recovered from the shock, I noticed that there were a number of iron chests in the corner of the room. They were locked shut, but the locks were so rusty that they gave way when I struggled with them for a bit.

I looked inside and saw gold, silver and copper coins in them. I grabbed a few and climbed out of the room. Then I ran to Nisha.

'Look what I found! Treasure!'

'That won't be of much use unless we can get out of here,' Nisha replied.

But suddenly, her eyes brightened and she beamed at me. I was a little alarmed by this change of expression.

'What happened?' I asked.

'Silver and copper coins! Do you realize what this means?'

'No,' I said curiously.

'It means we can finally get off this island! I can make a battery with this stuff!'

'Are you sure that will work?' I asked.

'It's worth a try.'

I watched as she took the coins and asked for the lemons I had picked earlier. She then disappeared into the forest for a while, saying that she needed some bamboo. I waited for an hour on the beach and was just about to go in after her when she emerged, carrying a bamboo tube with the coins inside. I watched as she took the radio out of her pocket and attached the wires in it to the tube. We waited in suspense for some time. Suddenly, we heard the crackle of static over the speaker.

'Hello?' Nisha yelled.

'Come in, Nisha. I hear you loud and clear,' said the voice on the other end.

We both desperately described our situation. After a pause, the person said, 'Your location has been tracked. Help is on its way.'

I heaved a sigh of relief at these words. We were finally going to be rescued.

a ring for mrs mehra

Aishwarya Mohandas, Age: 14, Kozhikode

Mrs Anupama Mehra was walking on air. With a sparkling diamond ring on her finger, she felt as if she owned the world.

The diamond on the ring was quite rare. It had come to India all the way from Africa. This one ring was enough to turn any pauper rich.

Mr Mehra was a leading industrialist. His company was among the top companies in India. So it is needless to say that the Mehras were very rich, and that they lived in a huge mansion on the outskirts of the city.

Mrs Mehra loved leading an idle and luxurious life. Her marriage to an industrialist had helped her a lot. Buying diamonds was her recent hobby. Diamond rings, necklaces and bracelets filled her jewellery boxes. But still she wanted more and more.

Ever since she had heard of this rare diamond from Africa, she had been insisting that her husband buy it for her. She was not bothered about the high price. She just *had* to own it. Mr Mehra loved his wife and always attended to her needs. So she got that ring on her finger.

That was not all. That night there was a huge party at Kalyan Gardens, where many eminent personalities and their families would be present. Mrs Mehra wanted to walk into the party wearing this diamond and become the main attraction of the evening. She wanted all the women to be jealous of her.

The doorbell interrupted her thoughts. She opened the door to find Nallappa standing there. Nallappa lived opposite their mansion in a small hut. He lived with his old mother, wife and children. He earned a living by collecting useful junk from households and reselling them. According to Mrs Mehra, the hut and its residents were an eyesore and a bad omen for their mansion.

Nallappa now told her that his mother was ill . He wanted to borrow some money for her treatment.

But Mrs Mehra was not one to fall for this. She said, 'Look Nallappa, your mother is sick now. Even if she gets better, she will be ill again sooner or later. Do you expect me to provide money every time this happens?'

Nallappa was speechless. He sputtered, 'But Memsaab…'

'Sorry Nallappa,' Mrs Mehra said plainly and shut the door on his face.

Nallappa walked back, heartbroken. He did not blame the memsaab, it was his fate. Otherwise, why should he have to collect junk to earn a living?

'Anupama, it's already time!' Mr Mehra's voice rang through the mansion later that evening. Mrs Mehra was all dressed up. Finally, she put the ring on her fingers and left for the party.

When she walked in, all eyes turned to the new guests. And no doubt, all eyes were on the ring on Mrs Mehra's finger. Mrs Mehra enjoyed all this thoroughly.

Whispers could be heard from the small groups of women here and there.

'Look, it's Anupama Mehra, and she's wearing a brand new diamond ring!'

'Well, she is very rich, what's the surprise in her wearing

a diamond ring?'

'No, I think it's special. I know diamonds when I see them.'

'Well, let's go ask her.'

'Mrs Mehra, you look stunning, and that ring is beautiful.'

'Oh yes. It's a rare kind, imported from Africa, you see.'

Back in the groups, the women whispered, 'Ugly little show-off!'

When it was dinnertime, everyone enjoyed the delicious buffet. Mrs Mehra finished her food and dropped the plate into the bin. When she went to wash her hands, she noticed something that nearly made her faint. Her ring finger was naked. The ring was missing!

Mrs Mehra felt as if she was melting into nothingness. 'My ring! Where is it! Who took it?' she screamed.

The search began for the ring. People looked everywhere—on the ground, near the food counters, even inside the food. Mrs Mehra was hysterical. She began accusing everyone of stealing the ring.

The next day, Nallappa was searching the junkyard. His mind was full of problems—his children's education, his mother's illness... Suddenly, he found something sparkling among the junk. A diamond ring! Nallappa had seen the memsaab wearing rings like these, and he knew that they were quite valuable. Who would throw out such a thing into the garbage?

Last night, as Mrs Mehra was dropping the plate, the ring had slipped off her finger and into the garbage bin. The garbage truck had carried it to the junkyard, where it reached Nallappa's hands.

In the mansion, Mrs Mehra was completely heartbroken.

It took her a few days to get over the loss. As she looked out of her window, she saw work going on at Nallappa's house. Was he going to reconstruct it? The pauper, who didn't even have the money to treat his mother? Mrs Mehra was left surprised and confused.

stargazing with nana

Nandita Bharadwaj, Age: 14, Chandigarh

I can see a wide blue ocean in front of me, the sun casting its glistening reflection on it. Tiny droplets of water are sprinkling my face, bringing with it a freshness in the air, and in me. The hot sun caresses my face as I close my eyes under its glare. Suddenly someone puts a soft, wrinkled hand over my eyes.

That hand I can still remember, though I was only four at that time and the rest of my memory is vague. Is it a miracle that I can still remember that hand so clearly? Well, no. It's just a simple recollection of a memory of someone whom you loved dearly and who has passed away, to take a place in the abode of God.

I told my grandfather, 'Oh Nana, it felt so lovely to have the sun on me...'

Nana looked at me lovingly and said, 'I know that, child, but I want the sun to touch your face softly.'

I let out a ponderous 'Oh'. I was just a child then, so I continued, in my child-like innocence, 'But Nana, the sun is so small, how can it touch me harshly?'

He replied, casting his eyes at the sun, 'It may appear small but it's powerful.'

My eyes grew wide as I discovered this new thing about the small, yellow sun. I asked him, 'Nana, is the sun more powerful than you?'

My grandfather laughed at my question. At that time I remember being a bit annoyed but now I understand the

reason for his laughter. He continued, 'Yes, my dear, it is more powerful than me.'

Losing no time I asked, 'Then how can you make the sun touch me gently?'

He looked straight into my eyes and said, 'Because he knows that I am your grandpa, and that I love you.'

I looked at him, he at me. He gave me a sudden hug. It was a special moment.

I said to him, 'Then put your hands over my eyes.' He did so gently. After a little silence, I asked abruptly, 'But what about the stars?'

'Oh, the stars! They are nice and far away. They just want to be looked at by everyone, appreciated by everyone. They bring smiles to everybody's faces, don't they?'

I agreed. 'Yes, that's why whenever I look at them I smile. I have to crane my neck to see them as they are far away.' He simply smiled. He took me in his arms and said, 'Let's go.'

I put my small hand around his broad shoulders and he started walking home. I looked back to see the waywardly moving waves of the ocean, and took a last look at the sky in the hope that the stars would come out. Then I looked down to see the shadow of him carrying me on the yellow sand.

Even as I write this, a smile flashes across my face. That moment with my grandfather has taught me a lot about respecting the small things in life. It has also taught me that you need small reasons to smile and be content with life. It has made me realize the splendidness of nature, its magnificence, its value. That's the reason why I still gaze at the stars and look at the sun. That picturesque scene from the beach comes alive in front of my eyes. Oh, that was indeed a lovely day!

how the donkey got a horn like the rhino

Ragini Dhar, Age: 11, New Delhi

Near the Kaziranga National Park lived a man with his donkey. The park was famous for the one-horned rhino. Each day, the donkey's owner would carry provisions for the park staff on the donkey. One day, the officer in charge of the park asked the man to bring three loads of bricks so that a small hut could be built for the park guards. These guards, the officer said, would then be able to keep watch night and day and prevent poachers from entering the park.

The next day, the man brought a load of bricks to the park. While he was unloading the bricks, his donkey was looking around. The donkey saw a rhino at a distance, walking slowly and eating shrubs. The rhino had a beautiful horn. Wondering how the rhino got the horn, the donkey slowly approached and asked, 'Mr Rhino, you have a beautiful horn. I wish I could have one like yours. Can you please tell me where I can get such a horn?' The rhino replied, 'Mr Donkey, I was born with the horn. As I grew older, the horn also grew bigger. There is no place from where you can get a horn. All of us in the park are born with our horns.' The donkey was not satisfied with the answer. He thought that the rhino did not want to tell him the secret of getting a horn.

The man brought another load of bricks to the park the following day. The donkey, spotted the rhino again and asked,

'Mr Rhino, you did not tell me yesterday the secret of how you got a horn. Please tell me how you got the horn. I also want a shining horn like yours. If I could get one all the donkeys would be jealous of me.'

Now the rhino was annoyed. He was feeling hungry and wanted to eat shrubs in peace but the donkey kept pestering him with his questions. So he told the donkey, 'Since you insist, I will tell you the secret of getting a horn. There must be a brick wall near where you live. Tomorrow morning, run fast and hit the wall with your head. You will have a nice horn on your head.'

The donkey was pleased to know the secret. Next morning, he ran fast and hit a brick wall with his head. Soon there was a big bump on his head. To him, it looked like the rhino's horn. There was, however, a problem. The bump hurt terribly. So he decided to see a donkey doctor. He told the doctor the entire story. The doctor listened patiently, smiled and said, 'I will tell you the cure. But before I prescribe it, I must get an X-ray of your head.' So the donkey's head was X-rayed in the doctor's laboratory. And what do you think they found? The donkey had no brain! The doctor smiled and said to the donkey, 'There is no medicine that can cure you. The only thing that you can do is to hit the brick wall again. That way you will have two horns instead of the one that rhinos have. You will be better looking than the one-horned rhino who gave you the advice.'

So the donkey hit the brick wall and soon, he got two bumps. Since then, he has been waiting for his master to take him to the Kaziranga National Park, so that he can show off his two bumps to the rhino.

the beauty of friendship

Sunreeta Bhattacharya, Age: 14, Kolkata

If each man is an island and the waters caressing his shores are sweet, the winds blowing over him are faithful, then let them be known as friends. Friends who bring with them good news and hope in times of trouble; friends who bring joy and cheer in good times. In times of monotony, they let the island know it is blessed, for now it has the time to rest and think of all that life has to offer. Such is friendship, the bond that links one heart to another with an invisible binding force, which exists across land and sea, where physical distance does not hinder the delicate spiritual companionship that friends enjoy.

When a child is born, his mother is all the world to him. Not a single breath escapes his mother's notice. The mother knows the baby better than anyone else and feels his aches and pains as her own. The baby does not know that there exists a world outside his mother's lap. As he grows, however, the world reveals itself to him, in all its varied range. The comparison between his physical reach and the vastness of the universe is often difficult for a growing child. All he needs to feel then is that he is not the only island in this vast ocean of civilization, and that there are others who share his feelings.

In nature, the little nestling out at play rejoices at the sight of another fellow bird and they catch worms together. It is a strange arrangement that the Creator has made for every creature. Though a man may be alone, his heart goes out to his fellow beings. A friendless person is a sorry sight to behold! There are good times and bad times in every man's life—spring, autumn, summer and winter—and all he needs is to share his life with a loved one. This is essential, so that he does not become too overwhelmed with life. Because, while happiness spreads when shared, sadness finds itself at a loss when many are there to partake of it. As we grow up, we come to realize that life's meaning lies hidden in the various situations we experience and that nobody is strong enough to walk the path of life alone.

Friendship, in its essence, is the assurance that an individual apart from yourself is there to listen to you, talk to you, to reciprocate your feelings of trust and faith in him. A friend knows you with all your virtues and your flaws, and loves you all the same. A friend can gauge your capabilities and identify the areas where you can shine. We all have role models in this world. Friends play an important role in moulding the future of a person; they can also be our role models. A friend can be a positive motivation and can stimulate constructive development in a person.

We have seen people who are friends of the masses. Gandhi, for example, evaluated the needs of his countrymen and strove for their fulfilment. We also have the example of Mother Teresa, who dedicated her life to the people who were underprivileged. She sacrificed her comforts willingly to bring smiles on their faces.

It is very crucial to recognize whether a friendship is constructive or not. Constructive friendship nourishes the soul and facilitates its growth. Narrow thoughts do not find any place in this form of friendship. A relationship that does not involve frankness, faith and mutual understanding is not friendship.

In the busy lives we lead, we need time to look into ourselves to discover truth and meaning. Time passes, what stays are our footprints—the outcome of our activities. Our lives influence others throughout this journey. Therefore, we must be careful in whatever we do, and share our experiences with a friend.

time travelling in a sack

Aditi Umashankar, Age: 12, Bangalore

Time travelling. It is something many people dream of. And who wouldn't? Just imagine the power of being able to go back to any time you want and to be able to change the events that occurred! But you could also end up creating serious problems. No, it is not only about the awful jet lag you'll get, but also the impossible things you'll end up doing. But wait, let me illustrate with an example. Let's just look at my travels back and forth in time. Yes, I'm a mad scientist, one of the many in the world, but the only one crazy enough to actually build a time machine.

The time machine I built was not exactly the sleek silver-and-bronze machine that you'd imagine, but instead, was a mouldy-looking sack. True, it was not one of the most gorgeous looking machines out there, but hey, at least I made one. Its functioning was simple. All you had to do was to climb in and speak in your clearest voice the time you wanted to travel to, while trying not to choke on the rank, damp smell inside the machine.

The first time I tried it, the time machine took me to a year far from what I had asked for. Let's just say I asked for the past, but I was taken to the future. The first thing that greeted me there was a big-eyed, furry ball on a metal spring. While I climbed out of the sack, muttering angry things about the time machine, the furry ball opened a mouth that didn't seem to exist before and sang squeakily,

'Iiin-iiin-intruuuder!' And that sounded like big trouble. By the time I managed to extract myself out of the time machine and fold and tuck it under my arm, the ball was surrounded by more of its kind. Each one of them started singing—if it could be called that—what the first ball had sung. The sound was ear-splitting and went on for five minutes. I was glad when it finally stopped. But my relief quickly faded when I spotted a gigantic big-eyed ball. It was twice as big as I was. I assumed it wanted assurance that I was harmless, so I picked up one of the smaller balls and started patting it. The master ball stared at me, opened its mouth and said in a squeakier voice, 'Down, intruder, down.' Then the ground opened up and swallowed me. I fell on a hard surface which felt like stone. It was pitch-black and I could not see anything. To add to my discomfort, the ball I had been carrying started headbutting me. I was fed up. I shoved the fur ball into my sack, went in after it and shouted, 'Take me to a time far away from this one!'

I guess I should have been more specific, because it took me to the Stone Age. This time, when I came out of the machine, there was no one to welcome me. I rolled up the sack and put it under one arm and the fur ball under the other. I started walking around, hoping I would not bump into any ferocious creatures. But of course, that's exactly what happened. After I had pushed my way through a thick patch of foliage, I came face-to-face with a dangerous looking man, with scraps of animal skin around his waist, dirty matted hair and an equally grimy beard. A cave man! He was standing slightly stooped, with an enquiring expression on his face as he squinted at me.

'Squeak!'

The fur ball had started to make its presence felt. It wriggled so much that I dropped it to the ground. It straightened up, gave me a scorching look, and turned around to face the man. It probably didn't have any common sense because it jumped right up to the man and proceeded to stare at him as if he was a naughty child. He quailed under its stare and started to look guilty. And then, trying to make amends for a non-existent mistake, he picked the ball up and started to scratch it. The ball made a purring noise and closed its eyes. The primitive man looked up at me, opened his mouth in an imitation of a smile and walked away, still scratching the fur ball.

I stood with my mouth agape. I had expected the cave man to pound the ball into goo, but instead the ball had bested him with a stare. Then they had become what looked like best friends and had gone away, leaving me alone. I was still bemused when I suddenly heard a roar somewhere near me. I was startled out of my thoughts. It didn't seem like a good idea to stay there after that sound, so I climbed into the sack and said, 'Take me back to where I started from.'

Fortunately, this time the machine obeyed and took me back to the present. I put the sack aside and sat down to ponder upon the effects of my time travel. If the furry ball now existed during the Stone Age, then where was it at present? I continued to think until I fell into a sleep filled with dreams of cave men and fur balls on springs.

the bitter truth

Neel Karia, Age: 14, Mumbai

In Heaven, Ram was conversing with Sita and Narad.

Ram: Sita, I have not been to Earth as a human in ages. This Women's Day, I received a lot of complaints from women. Will you be born on Earth again as a girl child?

Sita: That's brilliant. I would love to improve the condition of women on Earth. But how do I select my family?

Ram: Don't worry. We will give this duty to Narad.

Narad: Of course. I will fulfill this duty.

So Narad went to Earth in the disguise of a reputed fortune teller. He visited the slums to look for a mother-to-be for Sita. He spotted a Muslim lady. Narad was impressed with the lady's expressive eyes and soft voice. The lady came and bowed before him. Narad was happy to find out that she had been married two years ago and was hoping for a child.

Narad: Why have you come to me, woman?

Lady: Guruji, I have heard a lot about you and your powers of fortune telling. You know everything. If we receive a blessing from you, it is bound to be our destiny. So I have come here to seek your blessing.

Narad: God bless you with a wonderful baby girl.

Lady (surprised): Guruji, why are you blessing me with a girl and not boy? Don't you know that in our society, a girl is considered a burden?

Narad: But tomorrow's world will be a woman's world. Women will dominate in all spheres of life.

Lady: Guruji, I do not know about tomorrow. But today's world is miserable for women. I am the only daughter of my parents. They spent everything they had for my education and my marriage. Today, I earn but I have to give all my earnings to my in-laws. I cannot help my parents even if I wish to. I don't see any change in this society, at least not in the next generation. I don't want my daughter to experience all this.

Narad was puzzled. He decided to select some wealthy family instead to look for a mother-to-be for Sita. He visited a Jain temple situated in a posh area of South Mumbai in the disguise of a Jain muni. A woman had come to visit the temple with her five-year-old daughter. The girl spoke fluent English with her mother. As soon as they saw Narad, they both did the asthanga vandana. Narad started talking to the little girl. He was amazed to find out that the girl already knew five languages. She was learning classical dance and was a champion at skating. Just then, the girl joined other kids for the religion class that was held in the temple. Narad could hear the young girl narrating the shlokas in Prakrit. So Narad spoke to her mother.

Narad: I am impressed by the way you have brought up your daughter. I bless you with another princess.

Woman: Guruji, I already have a daughter. Now I want a brother for her. After all, we need a boy to continue our family line and perform our last rites.

Narad: I see Sita Maiyya in your next child. Your child will have a great influence on the world.

Woman: Thank you for your blessings, Guruji. But I don't want Sita Maiyya. She was abandoned by her husband Rama during her pregnancy in fact! Since then, women have always had to sacrifice for the family. My little daughter is

the Second sex
SWARG TIME
Dear God,

smarter than all the boys of her age put together, just as I was! But I will have to teach her to sacrifice her talents for her family. If I want a second child, I will now opt for the treatments available nowadays to ensure that the child is male.

Narad: But that's not ethical.

Woman: My sister has five daughters. Social pressure made her try for a sixth child in the hope of a boy. She finally delivered a baby boy. But she was so weak by the time of her sixth pregnancy that the child turned out to be mentally disabled. I don't want to go through that torture.

Narad realized that the task given to him was not an easy one. He decided to do a lot of research before meeting the next mother-to-be. He read that actresses like Sushmita had adopted two daughters, and that Mandira was looking forward to adopting a girl child. Narad felt that he should not lose heart. He decided to meet some more women instead: independent, successful women who worked in the media or in journalism. Finally, he found an actress who he thought would be perfect for the mother-to-be.

Narad: How do you feel about having a girl child?

Actress: I would have loved to have one but considering current events, I am a bit afraid. I am working, I can't take care of her all the time. But I will have to think twice before sending her anywhere with my driver. Our girls are not safe anywhere nowadays, not even in the school bus!

Narad could not take it anymore. At once, he left for Heaven.

Narad (to Ram): Lord, I think this is not the right time to send Sita Maiyya to Earth. Today, women are not safe in any continent, in any caste or class. But *you* must go urgently. Go and tell these selfish men that their wives are their biggest assets, and that to go to heaven you need your own good karma, not last rites performed by your sons.

Ram: Yes, Narad. You are right. I have set a wrong example. Now I will go and try my best to make up for my mistake. I will teach the world to respect women. Goodbye, Sita. I will see you after I complete my task.

eggs and patterns!

Anupama Ravichandran, Age: 15, Chennai

Brilliant white light came shining through and hit my eyes. Momentarily blinded, I pushed a tuft of hair out of the way and looked up. A blue sky greeted me and I gazed at it contentedly. The best thing about afternoon seistas in your backyard was the uninterrupted peace. Or so I thought!

Out of absolutely nowhere, I saw yellow dots floating in mid-air. They seemed to grow bigger as the seconds ticked by. They looked a pretty yellow, so I grinned at them happily, until one landed on my head!

The round objects were, in fact, eggs and they didn't stop coming! My athletic instincts kicked in and soon, I was running away from this 'yolk downpour' (as I like to call it), dodging the falling eggs and waving my hands madly.

Desperately, I searched for a place to take shelter and remembered my father's old tool shed. It was infested with every single species of creepy-crawlies and, under normal circumstances, I would have never dared to go in there alone. But now it seemed like paradise!

I threw open the shed door and flung myself in, closing the door quickly behind me. I breathed in deeply and turned on the lights. The place was exactly as I had always known it, but it didn't seem to retain its old scariness. In fact, it was surprisingly clean.

I wiped all the egg-mush off my face and hair. The sound of the 'yolk downpour' was still audible outside. Carefully,

I opened the door an inch and thrust my hand out in the hope of catching an egg. After all, I could at least make some good scrambled eggs while I was waiting. I hit jackpot and brought the bomb gently inside for further inspection.

It was an egg all right, but nothing near the usual ones. Its surface was dotted with weird patterns that were so minute and intricate that I couldn't help but admire the beauty of the artwork (completely forgetting how it had attacked me a few minutes ago). I rotated the egg in my hand slowly and observed it from every angle. I noticed that the faster I spun it, the more a pattern kept evolving on the surface of the egg, becoming clearer by the minute. Just as I was about to decipher the diagram, I thought I heard a raspy voice. I looked around the shed and scanned it thoroughly. There was no one to be seen.

'Not up there, human, turn your eyes downwards,' mumbled the raspy voice.

My first reaction was to drop the egg and run, and I wondered whether I was going insane and hearing non-existent voices.

'Your mental faculties are in perfect condition. Just do as I say,' the voice said.

Used to obeying orders, I glanced at my feet to find a large spider stroking my toes. I jumped, sending the spider ricocheting to the other side of the room.

This had to be a nightmare!

The spider painfully made his way back to me and implored, 'Listen to me, dear girl. I mean no harm. Trust in what you see.'

You wouldn't believe me if I told you this, but I felt sorry for the arachnid.

'Fine, but stand where I can see you,' I said nervously. The spider climbed on to a stool. He sighed and sang,

'The spiders of the world
Have come to know that you
Speak the tongue and word
That can solve an ancient clue.

We sought your attention
With the help of the birds
Who dropped their eggs in succession
On your head with aggression.

Now you speak with the representative
Of the great spider nation
Who stands alone like a stone
So as to not frighten you.

Don't deny us your knowledge
For history will remember you
As the great one who helped these commonly mistaken insects
Who cleaned a shed belonging to humans!'

I didn't know whether to be astounded by the fact that the spider spoke English or that it had managed to clean my father's shed! I was touched and decided to help this poor creature who had written a poem just for me.

Bending down to the spider's eye level, I whispered (if I spoke too loudly he would be blown away), 'So you want me to interpret the symbol on the egg?'

The spider replied with tears in his eyes, 'Oh yes! Oh yes! It contains a message that will help us catch more insects and flies.'

I didn't question the authenticity of his statement nor its meaning. I am a born puzzle solver and I set my mind to the task. When you love something, you do it with no questions asked!

The symbol was made up of concentric hexagons fitted neatly into one another with four water droplets on all sides. Everything I had ever read about the components of the symbol rushed through my mind and after what seemed like an hour, I finally cracked the code. Eureka!

Inspired by the spider, I answered his query in free verse. It went something like this:

'The hexagon your web, your domain
Is strong and smooth
Yet what you lack is trivial
and something you should have known.
The webs of your ancestors were extremely sticky
But yours lack the glue
Your lifestyle diseases like obesity and diabetes
Prevent insects from hanging on for long.
So exercise and work out
To improve your hunting from now on!'

The spider thanked me profusely and shook my hand (or at least, rubbed it) and bounced away. I stood gaping at the door with the egg in my hand. Spiders and humans have the same medical issues? I couldn't believe it!

Turning the egg in my hand again, I smiled at the patterns.

I should have guessed that only something as small as a spider could achieve such precision and style!

I could still hardly believe my mysterious adventure. I don't know how much of it was true and how much was imagined. But hey, just because it doesn't seem true, doesn't mean that it's not real!

www.ingramcontent.com/pod-product-compliance
Lightning Source LLC
LaVergne TN
LVHW091131080826
845145LV00008B/2116

* 9 7 8 8 1 2 9 1 2 9 3 3 8 *